THE
SHERLOCK
HOLMES
• MUSEUM •

MIND PALACE PUZZLES

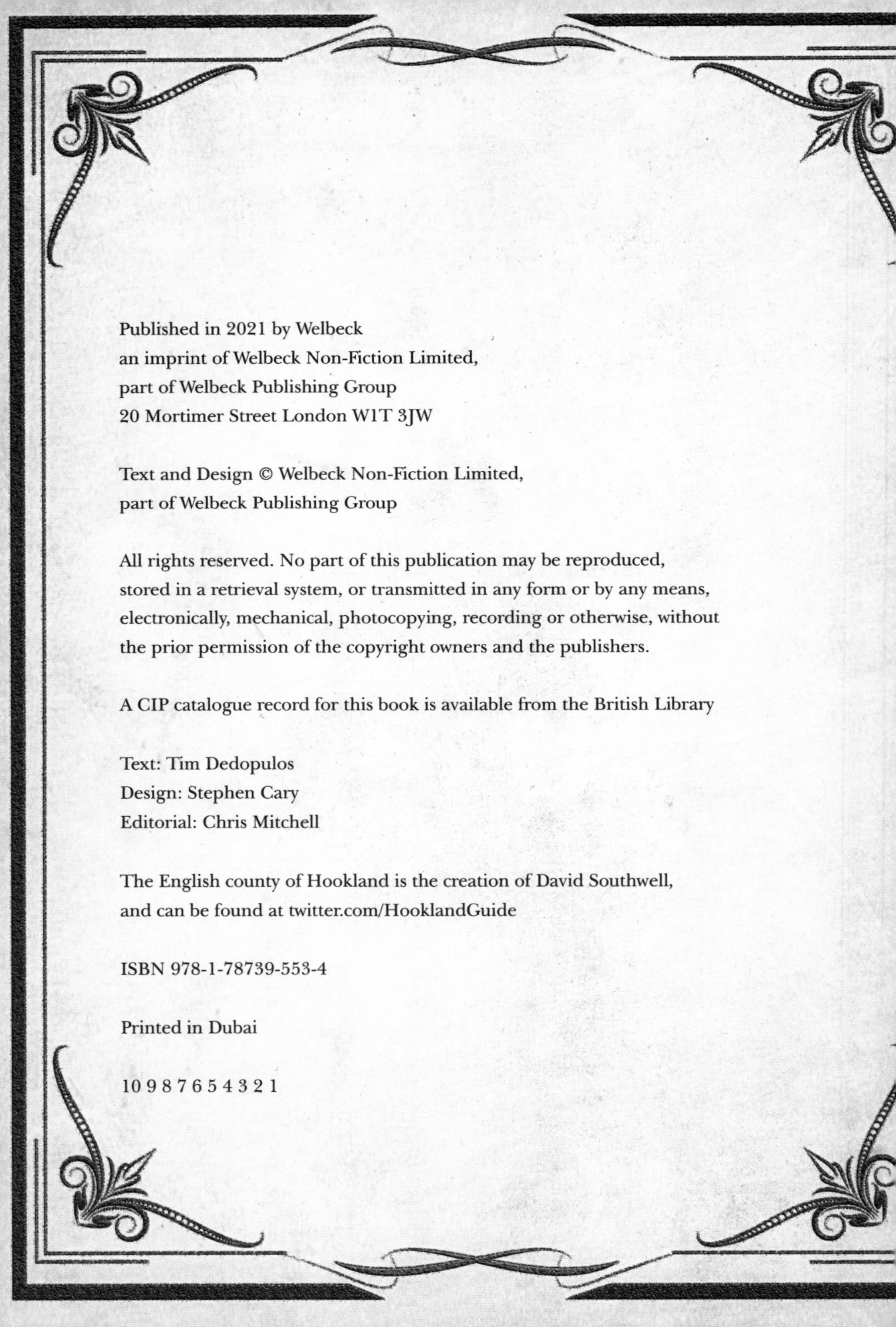

Published in 2021 by Welbeck
an imprint of Welbeck Non-Fiction Limited,
part of Welbeck Publishing Group
20 Mortimer Street London W1T 3JW

A CIP catalogue record for this book is available from the British Library

Text: Tim Dedopulos
Design: Stephen Cary
Editorial: Chris Mitchell

The English county of Hookland is the creation of David Southwell, and can be found at twitter.com/HooklandGuide

ISBN 978-1-78739-553-4

Printed in Dubai

10 9 8 7 6 5 4 3 2 1

THE SHERLOCK HOLMES • MUSEUM •

MIND PALACE PUZZLES

DR JOHN WATSON

CONTENTS

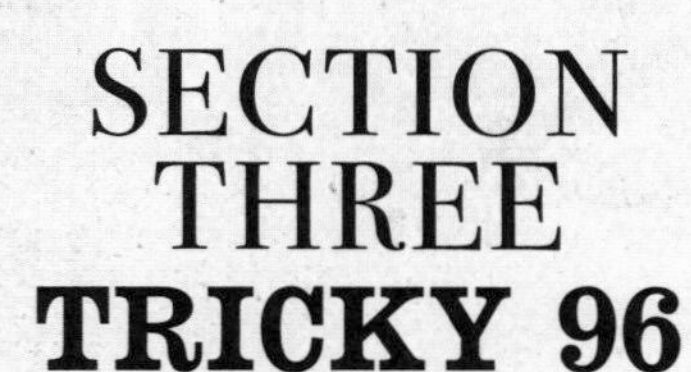

INTRODUCTION

My dear friend and companion, Sherlock Holmes, is a most singular person. He is undoubtedly the greatest detective in London, and it is my exceedingly strong suspicion that this accolade extends not only to the whole of the United Kingdom, but across the very face of the globe itself. I have travelled, in my time, and never met any soul his like.

Holmes's powers of observation are beyond remarkable. His ability to discern the most minute of details is far past being merely prodigious. A single glance is all that he requires in order to fully catalogue every nuance and particularity of any person, no matter how high or low their station. But this facility would hardly be the source of awe that it is were it not coupled to a truly incredible memory. For it is not enough to simply note that a particular whorl on a piece of ironwork is distinctive; one must also recall where else that whorl has occurred in order to understand what it implies. And it is here that the man's quintessential nature truly shines.

In honesty, the word "memory" barely suffices to describe Holmes's innate talent to retain information. Every sight, every sound, every texture, every sensory input that he experiences is sucked into the cavernous palaces of his mind, there to be stored and catalogued and teased apart, broken into significant pieces of information that can be cross-referenced as and when required. He is aided in this not only by a truly exceptional mind, but also by a number of fascinating techniques, which over time he has shared with me.

In these volumes I have prepared for you, I have assiduously attempted to pass on some of the mental exercises that Holmes has put me through. His aim has always been to strengthen my own meagre faculties for reason, creativity, logic, science, and arithmetic. This has not changed. I include many such examples within these pages.

On this occasion, however, I have also included, as best I can, the techniques of recall that Holmes has passed on to me – mnemonic visualisation, linking, loci, the Herigoné system of pegs, initialling, and more besides.

They are quite dazzling in their application.

So a portion of this volume is given over to the arts mnemonic and their practice. I promise you faithfully that these matters are not unduly complex, and, if put into use, will transform your memory. They have certainly transformed mine.

I hope, of course – as does Holmes himself – that the other mental exercises you will find in here will also help you to exercise and possibly even strengthen your mind. My personal experience of this process does definitely suggest that the analytical faculties can be sharpened with appropriate practice. But hope does not need to be employed in the matter of these memory techniques. They are entirely well-founded, and some have been in use since classical antiquity.

As always, I am in the matter of producing this volume nothing more than a humble scribe. However, I have done my best to arrange these puzzles and discussions into groups of complexity. This is something of a fool's errand – one man's difficult question is another woman's simple matter – but I have only my own indifferent mind by which to judge them. I am more confident that the memory practices build on one another, but even there, I beg your indulgence if you feel I am at fault.

My dear friends, it gives me a very great pleasure to present to you this third volume of the puzzles – and the Memory Palace – of Mr Sherlock Holmes.

I remain, in all ways, your servant,

Dr John Watson

Dr John H Watson,
221b Baker Street,
London NW1 6XE

SECTION ONE

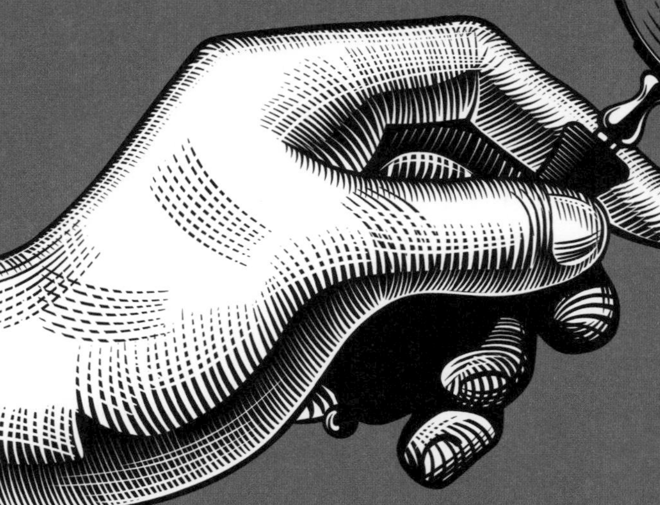

EASY

THE MEMORY PALACE

VISUALISATION

One afternoon, I made the error of complimenting Holmes on his exquisite memory. This was some months after his programme of seeking to improve my mind through the use of assorted questions had subsided. I had, in my naïveté, imagined that my comparative mental sharpness meant that I was out of those particular woods. Alas, it was not to be. My friend had merely been biding his time.

Rather than take my compliment in the spirit in which it had been intended, he made a disturbing pronouncement.

"My dear Watson, memory is a faculty that is quite straightforward to improve. I have been neglecting your mind of late. It is an important project, and I am returning to it as of now. Amongst my more typical trials, I shall include some exercises to sharpen your memory. Practise them diligently, and I solemnly promise that even you will be astonished at the results."

He was absolutely correct, naturally, and I wish I'd known his exercises when I was a medical student. I shall therefore include his comments and exercises in this volume, along with his more typical

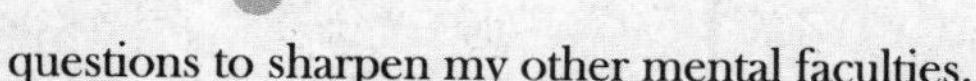

questions to sharpen my other mental faculties.

His first small lecture was about the ways that memory functions, and I repeat it as close to verbatim as I am able.

You need to know a few basic principles, old chap. Firstly, the memory beds in because of recall, not repetition. If you force yourself to remember something correctly, the brain interprets that as a signal of importance, and makes it easier to remember next time.

Secondly, for the great majority of people, images are more readily remembered than sounds or sensations. We recall scenes more accurately than text.

Thirdly, unusual or charged events are more memorable then regular ones. Absurdity, sexuality, and violence will always be the easiest to recall. The mind places the least importance on routine events.

Finally, our mind is only able to hold a few items consciously at one time – half a dozen or so. If you have ever needed to remember a list of groceries, this will be deeply familiar to you. This shortcoming needs to be accounted for.

The best way to remember a single point of information is to visualise a pictorial scene that both reminds you of the datum and is powerfully charged. This means coming up with a powerful image, a mnemonic, that will remind you of the piece of information in question. It will not help you to recall elephants if your image is of the door of 221b, old chap. Not unless your mind is considerably more curious than I suspect, anyway.

As a rule of thumb, the mnemonic that your mind first suggests to you will usually be your best bet. You will never reveal your mnemonics to any living soul, so do not be afraid, in the privacy of your own mind, to make them as shocking as seems fit.

Remember that memory learns through recall. Once you have picked an image and concentrated on it for a moment or two, banish it, and then recall it and, through it, the piece of information you wanted to remember. Continue to do this repeatedly, but space these repetitions out with increasing time. One hour, two, four, eight, a day, two days, four days, and so on. As you persist, the information you seek to perfect will bed down ever more strongly in your mind.

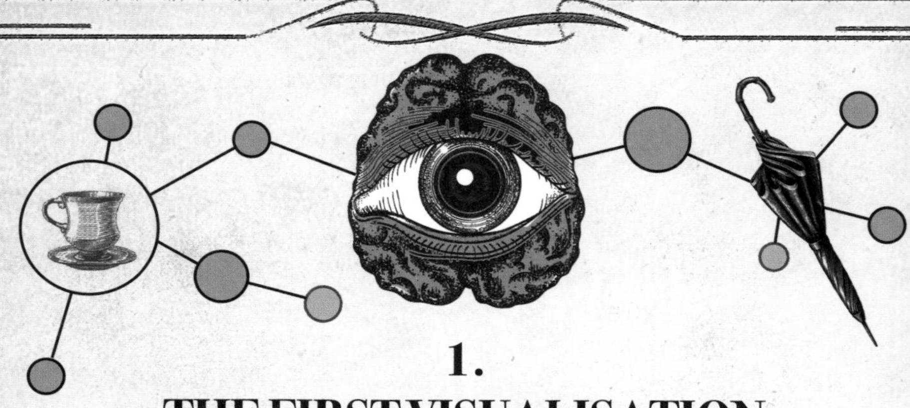

1.
THE FIRST VISUALISATION

"Now that we've gone over the foundational principles of how the memory functions, I think we ought to try a little demonstration. Don't you?"

I sighed. "Capital idea, Holmes," I managed.

He wasn't fooled of course. "Don't worry, Watson. This first time, I'd like you to set yourself up for failure. I'm going to tell you something that I want you to make into a mnemonic image which you will then attempt to remember. However, I want you to choose a mental picture that is as ordinary and tedious as you can possibly make it."

"I see," I said doubtfully.

"The idea is to demonstrate the issues involved in lacklustre mnemonic images. For example, I have noticed that you have your cup in that precise location on the table around sixty per cent of the time, so if I were to pick 'oolong tea' as your test, imagining your cup in that position would be ideal. Or if I were to pick, say, 'rain', then your umbrella in its habitual position in the umbrella stand by the door would be a suitable mnemonic for our purposes."

I nodded. "Bland thoughts."

"Precisely. Now, the datum that I wish you to remember is butter, and, on this occasion, I would encourage you to not practise recalling your deliberately tedious mnemonic image, but merely to focus on it briefly and then let it go."

I did so. Will you?

SOLUTION ON PAGE 176

THE COLLECTOR

One morning, whilst reading *The Times*, I came upon a brief article mentioning the death of one William Cavendish, a fellow of some wealth who, it said, had been a noted collector and patron of poetry. The writer who had prepared the article had clearly not done much research, describing the deceased's collection of first edition volumes of poetry as consisting of fewer than fifteen hundred volumes, but, then, in the very next paragraph, putting this total at more than fifteen hundred volumes. The cause of death was given as accidental.

Holmes walked past, saw what I was looking at, and tutted. "That Cavendish story is utter nonsense. Apart from the fact of his death, it didn't get a single thing right. He wasn't a patron or a collector, he was a publisher of poetry. He was murdered, of course, for some substantial debts he'd fallen into. Lestrade will get there in a day or two." He paused, and turned to look at me with a sardonic air. "I'm sure you now understand how many volumes were in his first edition library, naturally."

"Naturally," I said, and returned to the page.

How many first editions did Cavendish have?

SOLUTION ON PAGE 176

3

RAINBOW

Holmes and I were crossing Regent's Park late one afternoon, returning to Baker Street after some fruitless investigations in St John's Wood. We came across an alderman and a very rum bucket of live trout, but that is not of immediate relevance. The day had been rather wretched, although a brisk easterly was now clearing the overcast. As we approached the nursery, I happened to glance towards King's Cross and spotted a particularly magnificent rainbow set against the retreating dark of the clouds.

I pointed it out to Holmes, who looked across at it and nodded to himself. "You know, I trust, that the effect is caused by light refracting through water droplets."

"Of course," I said indignantly.

"Why do you not always see a rainbow when light is directly shining on water droplets, then?"

That one I had to think about for a moment.

Do you know the answer?

SOLUTION ON PAGE 176

4

CROSSING

The case of the bewildering banker was an irksome affair, at least for me. Holmes seemed to find it all vaguely amusing, although I couldn't begin to tell you why. We spent an inordinate amount of time loitering on malodorous docksides in inclement weather. I don't mind the sea, it can be quite soothing, but I'm not a great fan of ships or their ports.

On our fourth evening at St Katharine Docks, Holmes decided to spring another of his little challenges on me.

"I happen to know that there is a company running daily cruise liners between Southampton and Manhattan Island, leaving in both instances at noon, Greenwich Mean Time." Holmes told me.

"Oh?" I asked. I had not, at that point, realised that this was unrelated to our case.

"The crossing takes exactly one week, give or take a few minutes."

"It's amazing how fast these new liners are getting," I said.

He ignored that. "Let us say that you were taking that journey. How many of the company's liners would you encounter coming the other way, not including the one that is pulling in to Southampton as you depart?"

My answer was not correct. Can you do better?

SOLUTION ON PAGE 177

5

MOUNTAIN TIME

Being an Englishman, I am fortunate in that I do not have to worry overmuch about mountains. I did quite enough of that in Afghanistan. Since leaving the military I have permitted them to fade in my memory into distant things – pretty enough, but best viewed from a respectable distance, gin in hand.

So I was not entirely delighted when Holmes informed me, out of the blue, that he wanted me to think about the things as part of his ongoing efforts to sharpen my mental acuity.

I put down the novel I had been reading. "If I must," I replied. I admit I was a touch grudging about it.

"Is it cold in the mountains?" he asked me, his expression innocent.

I blinked at him a couple of times. "You know damn well it is, Holmes."

He smiled, a predatory glint in his eye.

"Why?"

SOLUTION ON PAGE 177

FEATURED

"It cannot have escaped your notice, Watson, that we are broadly symmetrical."

That pulled me up sharpish. Physically, Holmes and I are not much alike. He is taller than I, with a long face and a thin build that hides a surprising amount of wiry strength. I am of a comfortable shape nowadays, and while I'm still reasonably strong, no-one would have accused me of being designed for athletic endeavour, even before my leg became problematic.

He shook his head at my expression. "Humans, Watson. Humans. Not you and I."

"Oh, I see. Yes. Nature is thrifty. A degree of symmetry minimises points of wear and tear on the frame."

"Quite," he said. "But as you say, nature is thrifty. I was thinking of organs. Do you see a clear benefit to two eyes, or is one just there as a backup? What about ears? We do fine with one mouth. Or internal organs, for that matter? There's just one heart, one liver, one stomach, but two lungs and two kidneys. Do we need those?"

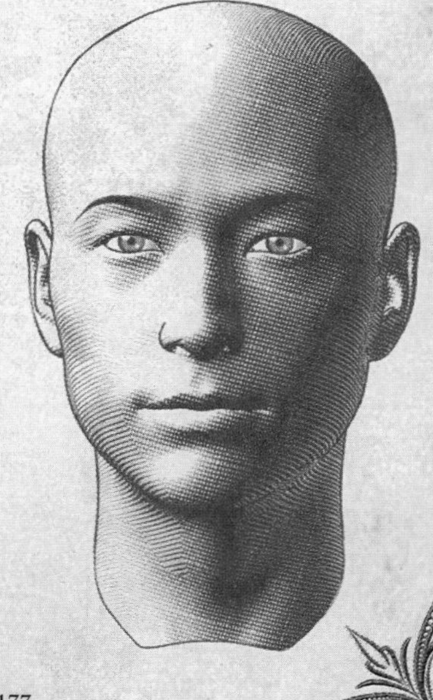

It's trivial for a doctor to answer, of course, but I suspect Holmes intended me to pass the question on, so what do you think?

SOLUTION ON PAGE 177

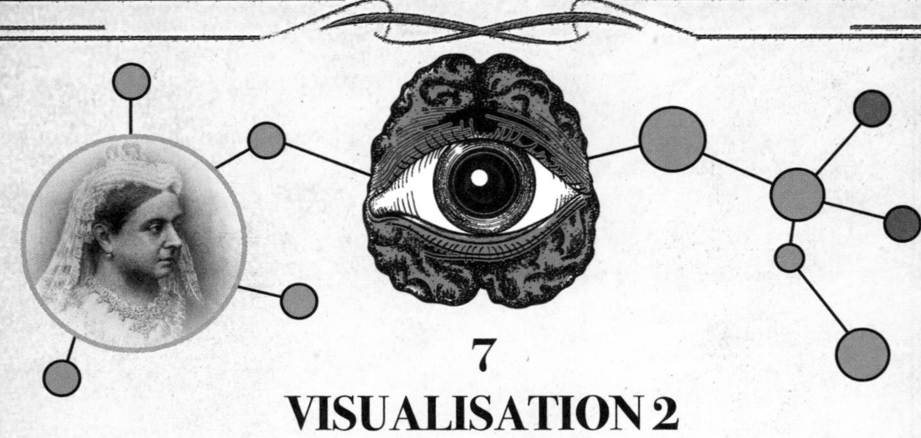

7
VISUALISATION 2

Can you recall the image I asked you to construct in your mind a short time ago, and what it was supposed to remind you of?

It was a couple of days after Holmes's initial discourse on the nature of memory when he interrupted my boiled egg to demand, "What piece of information did I ask you to remember?"

In fact, I did not even remember entirely to what he was referring. I flailed for a long moment, thinking about our recent cases, before making the association to memory in the abstract. It was several long seconds further before I was able to recall correctly the mental image I had made.

"Good, Watson," Holmes said. "This is an important first step. If I had just made mention of the datum to you in passing, with no unusual emphasis, I think it fair to say that you would not have been able to recall it at all at this point."

"I'm certain you're right," I admitted.

"Still, you visibly had to reach. So for the next test, let's put our notion of emotional charge to work. Relying on the principles of absurdity and so on, I want you to focus for a moment on a mnemonic image of Queen Victoria. Do so in good conscience, free of all guilt. The precise substance of your mnemonic will never be shared."

SOLUTION ON PAGE 178

8

SECURITY CONCERNS

Holmes and I were investigating an unlikely theft at a firm named DDM Partners. It so transpired that DDM was not an abbreviation, but the initials of the surnames of the three partners.

Someone had stolen a considerable amount of papers and bonds from the firm's safe but, apparently, without disturbing or mutilating any of the highly secure locks that held the safe shut. The keys were exclusively held by the partners, each of whom had an excellent and entirely independent alibi for the time of the robbery.

What made the case interesting to my dear friend was the nature of the safe. It was highly advanced, but the curious part was the arrangement of the keys. With a unusual degree of ingenuity, the partners had devised a system whereby any two of them together could open the safe, but one alone could not.

Can you figure out the system?

SOLUTION ON PAGE 178

CARL ÄDE
PATENT
STUTTGART
BERLIN
PATENT
C.ÄDE

EDNA

I have long suspected Mrs Hudson of being in cahoots with Sherlock in regard to the matter of my supposed improvement. Her implausible anecdotes regarding her extensive family flourished at about the same time that he stopped randomly firing questions at me, and the coincidence was something of a stretch to my credulity. My suspicions firmed into dreadful certainty when, a few days after his first memory discussion, she paused after bringing up some tea to offer another preposterous yarn.

"My aunt Edna is getting on a bit, Doctor," she informed me.

I nodded non-committally, expecting a tale of bunions or some such affliction.

"I think she believes she's getting younger."

"Ah," I said. That's never a good sign.

"Yes," Mrs Hudson said. "She told me just the other day that she is four times as old now as I myself am, but that five years ago, she was a full five times as old as I then was."

"Ah," I repeated, the unpleasant penny starting to drop.

She smiled at me, a picture of perfect innocence. "Of course, that could tell you my age, but you're far too much the gentleman to do such a thing to me."

She departed, and I caught a glimpse of amusement on Holmes's face.

Can you calculate her supposed age?

SOLUTION ON PAGE 178

10

THE WANDER

"There's an interesting little titbit in here that might amuse you," Holmes told me one afternoon. He was brandishing a periodical at me, one of his interminable volumes that he compulsively absorbs to keep fully informed.

"Oh?" I asked.

"Yes. It recounts that the son of a mariner, a young man on the cusp of adulthood, rather surprised his parents one afternoon when he declared that he was going for a lengthy wander, but he would be back before dawn. The surprise was not that he was going, or in his keeping his word and returning duly, but that when he left he was clean-shaven, and when he returned he had a perfectly natural beard, thick and bushy, grown normally."

"My word!"

"Quite."

Can you imagine how this might have transpired?

SOLUTION ON PAGE 179

CLOCK, WISE

One lunchtime, I looked up from my herring to check the time on Holmes's grandfather clock, an elegant fixture of the room. He's never mentioned where he acquired it, but he has had it as long as I've known him. It's extremely accurate, but then if that were not the case, it would never have survived in his possession. It was sixteen minutes past one, in case you were curious.

Holmes followed my gaze. "Clockwise," he mused. "The way that the clock invariably turns. Why is that the standard for the movement of a clock's hands, rather than widdershins, or something entirely different? It did not happen arbitrarily, not in the least. What do you imagine, Watson?"

I glumly imagined my herring getting cold, but I did not vocalize that fact.

Can you work out the answer?

SOLUTION ON PAGE 179

SHANE

"Mrs Hudson was telling me about her nephew, Shane, earlier," Holmes said, apropos of nothing.

We were on the south bank of the Thames, looking across at the Houses of Parliament. Lestrade had developed some wild theory about the lethally dangerous potential to infiltrate Parliament from the river, and was desperate for Holmes's evaluation. My friend agreed to oblige the Inspector solely because there was a new pottery operating in the near vicinity, and he wanted to get a look at the clays that they were using.

Taking my lack of immediate reply as a sign to press on, Holmes continued. "She asked me to inform you that each of his children has at least one brother, and each of his children has at least one sister. I trust you see the immediate implication?"

What is the smallest number of children in the family?

SOLUTION ON PAGE 179

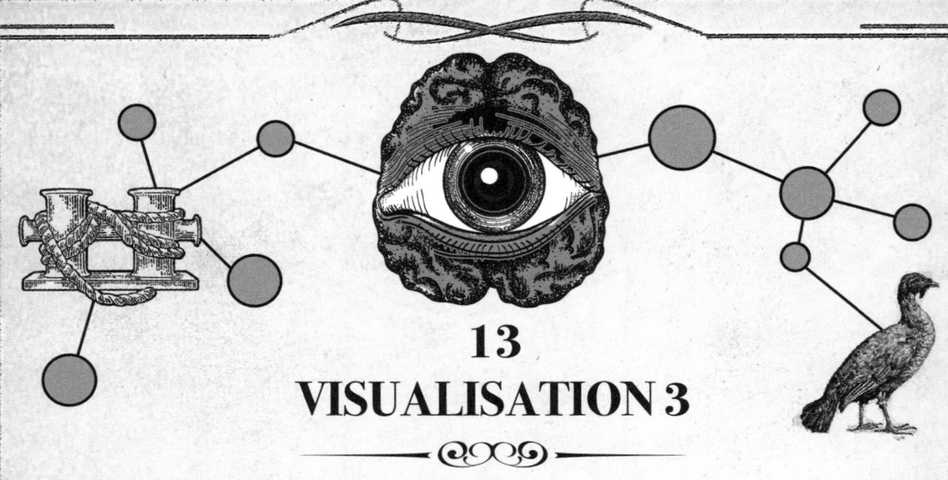

13 VISUALISATION 3

Can you recall what I asked you to remember last time?

When Holmes tasked me with recalling the second image I'd constructed, he was no less obtuse than on the previous occasion, but this time I immediately discerned his intent, and it took little effort on my part to provide the correct answer.

Holmes nodded in satisfaction. "You will note that this was easier."

"Yes," I said. "But I suspect that this was, at least in part, due to it not being the first of these little memory tests."

He smiled at that. "Exactly, my dear Watson. Exactly! Practice of recall is what solidifies the memory as important. The simple fact of having been put in this position on a previous occasion helps you this time. The comparatively vivid image also serves to provide substantial assistance. Both elements are important. The memory builds upon itself."

I nodded.

"So this time, when I give you your assignment, I want you to form a charged image for it in your memory. Then I would like you to distract yourself for twenty seconds or so – read a bit of that paper – before stopping to recall the image a second time, and then to repeat the process with a slightly longer gap, say a minute, before recalling it a third time. So prepare a mnemonic image for the city of Glasgow, and then go about your process of recalling it to help it bed in."

SOLUTION ON PAGE 180

URIE
PHOTOGRAPHER

14

STRAIGHT ACROSS

Holmes and I were walking down Cheapside one afternoon during our investigations into the Case of the Alderman's Trout. It was the first pleasant day we'd had after an extended period of rain, and the streets were unusually clean and fresh.

As we passed an apparently unremarkable tailor's shop, Holmes drew my attention to his sign.

"Observe the shape of this fellow's board, old chap. A little too wide to be a square, bisected into a pair of uncomfortable-looking triangles. And over there, that chandler next to the pub, his lenticular logo might look like an eye if that vertical stroke wasn't dividing it into two halves."

"Curious," I said.

"History surviving into modernity," Holmes said airily. "But I want you to think of the bisecting line at the moment. It should be clear that, for both these signs, any line chopping its shape into two halves of equal area will always pass through one common point, at the precise centre."

I thought about it. "Yes, that makes sense."

"So is that true for all flat shapes?"

SOLUTION ON PAGE 180

15

FLAGSTAFF

"I'd like you to think of a flag, Watson."

I sat up a little straighter, obediently called the Union Jack to mind, and nodded.

"It will not have escaped your notice that flags ripple in the wind, even if there are no buildings or trees in the immediate vicinity to cause air disturbance. Think of a pennant on a tower, or a flag outside of a fort."

"Indeed so."

"I'm sure you know that eddies and whirls in the wind are the result of local topography. The wind itself often changes direction, but it does so at a stately pace. Even the changes in wind direction caused by a tornado passing by are slow compared to the ripples of a flag. Flags always ripple, even the silkiest ones, but weather vanes do not twitch back and forth. The wind itself does not ripple. So why do flags do so?"

That set me pondering.

What do you think?

SOLUTION ON PAGE 180

16

LYNN

I was contentedly examining the weekend's cricket scores one morning when Holmes thrust a different newspaper under my nose. I recoiled in reflexive horror, getting enough distance from it for the masthead to resolve into the *Eastern Daily Press.*

"Here's a little something interesting out of King's Lynn," Holmes announced, pulling the paper back as I reached for it. "Permit me to summarise."

"Of course," I managed.

"On Tuesday lunchtime, a farmer by the name of Stephen Meyers discovered a fellow hung in a tree on the border of one of his fields, quite dead. It had snowed the previous afternoon, and he could see that the ground around the tree was quite undisturbed, so rather than approach, he called the police. They poked around, decided that the victim, an Oxfordshire man, had been dead for twelve hours, and ruled the death as accidental."

"Oh," I said.

Holmes nodded. "For once, I am in perfect agreement with Norfolk's finest. I am, of course, withholding one simple fact that explains the situation quite adequately."

"What do you imagine it is?"

SOLUTION ON PAGE 181

COLD

Holmes and I were on Regent Street, loitering opposite a rather upscale jeweller's establishment and hoping to get a glimpse of the Bewildering Banker's mistress. I had not been informed as to precisely why he and I both had to be there, or, indeed, why we had not passed the task on to Wiggins, who is far better suited for these things than I. As it was, the jeweller's doorman was watching us with deep suspicion, broken only by an occasional sneeze.

After one particularly thunderous offering audible even across the busy street, Holmes turned to me. "Correct me if I am wrong, doctor, but my understanding is that influenza is primarily seasonal in Europe, yet year-round in the tropics."

"That's broadly true," I said. "It's more prevalent in tropical areas during monsoon season, but yes, it is a mostly winter disease here."

"If our warmer summers inhibited the disease, or gave us extra resistance to it, you'd expect the tropical areas to be free of it most of the time, yet they are not."

"Indeed," I said, wondering where he was going with this line of enquiry.

He nodded.

"So why is it seasonal here?"

SOLUTION ON PAGE 181

18

TRIBALITY

Holmes was tossing a chess piece from hand to hand, a white bishop, seeming entirely careless of it but nevertheless catching it perfectly each time. After a little while, he noticed my attention, and waved it at me.

"My dear Watson," he said, his voice a touch grandiose. "I trust you recall occasions in the past where I have bedevilled you with questions regarding entirely theoretical peoples divided into two binary opposing tribes, obligate liars and obligate truth-tellers."

I nodded unenthusiastically. "I do indeed."

"Well, I'd like you to ponder a different sort of entirely theoretical divided people for me, those who are incorrect in their every thought and opinion, and their opposites, those who are correct in all their beliefs. They refer to the tribes as 'Wrong' and 'Right'. Fortunately, we can assume both Wrong and Right are telling you the truth, as they understand it."

"Sounds ghastly," I said.

"So let us suppose that you are faced by a pair of these people, ones about whom you know nothing more than I have already explained. The one on the left, whose name is Bill, steps forward and tells you, 'We are both Wrong.' His companion's name, as it happens, is Mick."

"Which tribe, or tribes, do the pair belong to?"

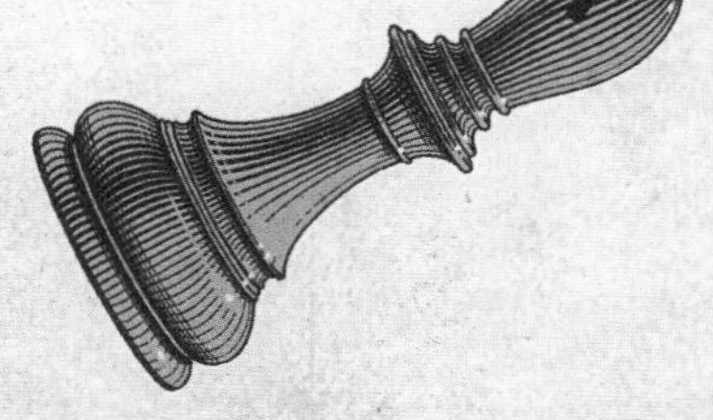

SOLUTION ON PAGE 181

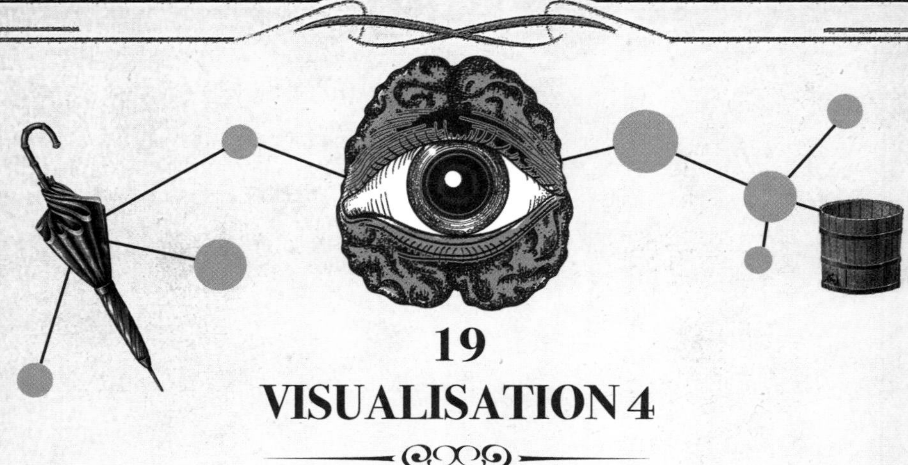

19
VISUALISATION 4

Can you recall what I asked you to remember last time?

When Holmes demanded out of the blue that I recall his third mnemonic, I actually found that the answer came to my tongue quite swiftly. We were on Marylebone High Street at the time, but the controlled chaos around us did little to distract my recall.

"You're doing well," he told me. "You're a long way behind Wiggins still, but that's only to be expected."

"I say, old chap," I protested.

Holmes cut me off. "No slight intended, my dear Watson. I have been training the Irregulars in these techniques for two years now. You'll catch up."

"Hrm," I grumbled.

"Take heart! One more practice of forming a mnemonic image, and we will move on to meatier fare. Being as lurid and emotionally potent as possible again, I want you to form a mnemonic for rain. As you did last time, think about something else for a short period of time before recalling your mnemonic, and then again after a somewhat longer interval. On this occasion, however, I will prompt you to recall your memory without revealing it to me on a few occasions over the next day or two."

I shall endeavour to replicate this effect in the pages of this book.

SOLUTION ON PAGE 182

MEMORY PALACE
BEFORE GOING ANY
FURTHER, PLEASE TAKE
A MOMENT TO RECALL
THE LAST MNEMONIC
I ASKED YOU TO FORM.

20

LUNACY

As time passes, I find that my appetite for skulking around in the night-time wanes noticeably. Nevertheless, much malfeasance is conducted under cover of darkness, and so it is inevitable that from time to time Holmes will need me to accompany him on some nocturnal errand or other.

We were crossing Clapham Common one chilly night, heading towards a pub on the south side in the hopes of getting a look at a particular nefarious haberdasher's co-conspirators. The moon had long-since set, and the common was really quite dark. I made some offhand comment about how useful a bit of moonlight might have proven.

Holmes nodded sagely. "The new moon was yesterday, so it would have been of little help. But tell me, old chap. When you look at the shining crescent of the new moon, sometimes you can almost see the rest of the face despite its darkness. Is that an illusion offered up by memory?"

What do you think?

SOLUTION ON PAGE 182

WATERY CAN

"I have a little thought experiment for you, my dear Watson." Holmes was sat in his usual chair, fingers steepled.

I set down my newspaper, and nodded.

"Imagine there is a jar with a couple of small holes close together near the bottom. The jar is filled with water, so naturally small streams of it are leaking out of the holes. If you fit a tight lid onto it, the leaks will stop. When you remove it, the leaks will resume. That is one effect."

I nodded again. "So far, so good," I said.

He gave me an odd look. "Quite. Now, if you were to move your finger back and forth through the streams of leaking water, the streams would merge and when you removed your hand, they would stay merged. That is the other effect."

"Sounds plausible, old chap."

"You are in a strange mood today, my dear Watson. I encourage you to try it for yourself. In the bathroom, though, You don't want to set Mrs Hudson on the warpath."

"An excellent point. I may give it a whirl. Or a stir at the least."

Holmes arched an eyebrow.

"In the meantime, I wonder if you could tell me what you imagine is responsible for each of the effects?"

SOLUTION ON PAGE 182

BISCUITRY

MEMORY PALA

Before going any further, please tak a moment to recal the last mnemonic I asked you to form

Inspector Lestrade was at 221b, having come to consult Holmes on the apparently vexatious matter of the death of the publisher William Cavendish. It took my dear friend all of forty seconds to explain that Cavendish had been murdered by debtors, and to get the Inspector to understand how, and which individuals were most likely responsible.

Caught between delight and despondency at Holmes's mastery of the situation, the Inspector put a considerable dent in Mrs Hudson's plate of biscuits while he finished his tea, and after we had suffered his effusive gratitude, departed.

Holmes turned to me as the door closed. "It may have escaped your notice that Lestrade had three times as many biscuits as you did, Watson."

I thought about it for a moment. "I wasn't really paying close attention, I'm afraid."

"Well, let us say that I, in turn, had half as many as you did."

"Very well, old chap. As you like. I doubt you spoiled your luncheon either way."

"And," he said, a trifle pointedly, "if we imagine that the good Inspector devoured eight more biscuits than you did, what would that tell you about my biscuit consumption?"

Can you figure out the solution?

SOLUTION ON PAGE 183

METEORIC

During the Nasty Business with the Onion Barrel, Holmes and I had reason to spend an afternoon wandering back and forth in Victoria Park, past Bethnal Green. It is a lovely space, and a vital opportunity for the residents of the East End to actually spend some time in a natural environment. On that particular afternoon, however, it had been raining prodigiously, and the experience was muddier and less conducive to lifting my spirits than usual.

As we came around the bathing pond for the third time, Holmes pointed out a long scrape in the mud. "See the edges of that impact, Watson? That pattern is definitive of a thrown half-brick. From the length of the scrape, I'd say it was flung by a ten-year-old, and he was clearly aiming – ineffectually – at a mallard."

"Clearly," I said.

"Now, if you look at the literature surrounding meteors – Ensisheim, for example – you will inevitably discover that they are said to leave circular craters behind. However, it should be clear that meteors do not typically strike the Earth square on. They are almost always said to streak through the sky, and the odds are significantly with that being the case. So why do they produce circular craters and not long, streaking ones such as the one over there?"

That stumped me for several minutes.

What do you think?

SOLUTION ON PAGE 183

24

A DISPLACEMENT

Holmes and I were discussing Basingstoke one morning when, apropos of nothing, he whipped a closed leather pouch out of the pocket of his smoking jacket and waved it at me. "Do you know what is in this pouch, Watson?"

My mind boggled for a moment. "I have absolutely no idea, old chap. Should I?"

"Definitely not. However, please believe me when I tell you that it is equally likely to contain either a small white ball, or a black ball that is distinguishable from the former only by its colour."

The pouch looked suspiciously flat to me, but I merely said, "Very well."

"Capital," Holmes said. "Now please imagine that I am adding a further indistinguishable ball to the pouch, this one most certainly white. At this point, the pouch contains two balls, one certain, one uncertain. Afterwards, I close the pouch, shake it around, and then remove one ball. The ball I remove is white. I discard it."

"Duly imagined, my dear Holmes. You were most deft in your movements, although I'm not sure how this relates to Basing House."

"Do try to keep up, Watson. How likely is it that the ball remaining in the pouch is white?"

SOLUTION ON PAGE 183

Linking

This was the second of Holmes's short lectures on the techniques of memory improvement. Once again, I shall endeavour to reproduce his comments word for word.

Now that you have a grasp of how to go about remembering a single point of information, my dear Watson, it's time to try your hand at multiple items. The brain has a limit as to how many things it is capable of keeping immediately to hand – just seven, give or take a couple depending on the person and their levels of fatigue and stress.

So remembering multiple items presents a challenge. Fortunately, there are ways to use the mind's internal structure to our advantage. You see, at a very deep level, we run on stories. Even now, most of us still understand the world through the stories we tell ourselves, and even though we may never be consciously aware of our internal stories, we take great exception if they are challenged.

Stories help us remember.

If you want to remember a list of things, you have to use that list to tell a story, and you do that by concocting mnemonic associations from each

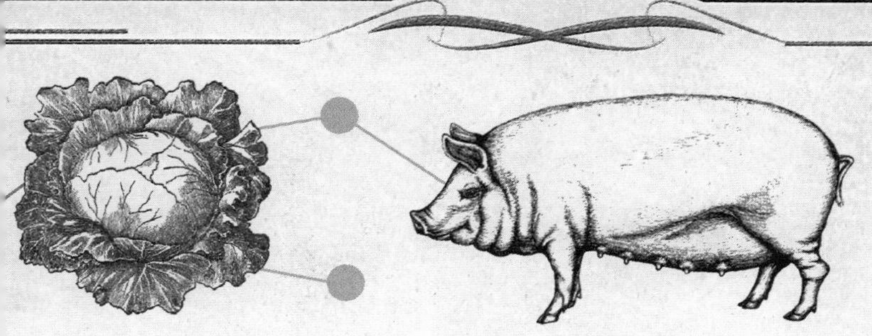

item to the next. This is known as "linking". Recalling the first mnemonic introduces the first item. The next moves you from the first to the second, then from the second to the third, and so on for an arbitrarily long list.

So, for example, a cabbage falling out of a cloud and striking a policeman on the head might be a suitable image for a list starting with cabbages. Say, then, the cabbage explodes and a dancing bee rises out of it, to remind you of honey. The bee flies over to a pigsty and stings a pig in the belly, to bring bacon to mind. And so on. Each image flows into the next. An incoherent story, perhaps, but still a story.

Not every datum provides a ready image, of course. What if you need to remember a long number, or an abbreviation, or a foreign name you have not previously encountered? Abbreviations are easy, if you follow Sir Isaac Newton's example of ROYGBIV, or "Richard Of York Gave Battle In Vain", for the colours of the rainbow. Use the letters as initials of a sentence with, yes, some story to it.

Numbers are but a little trickier. You need to break them into pieces that have some meaning for you, and then use those meanings as seeds of your mnemonics. For instance, I would find the number 54184722151023 trivial to remember – 54 is the year of my birth and 1847 the year of Mycroft's, 221 the address of this apartment, 5'10" the height of Langdale Pike, and 23 the number of urchins currently working with Wiggins. Ingenuity is your friend.

For everything else, you have a couple of options. Either treat the datum (or its name) as an abbreviation, or else create a mnemonic for something else which starts with the same few letters – thus, to remember the Bohemian poet Vítezslav Hálek, you could create mnemonics for vittles and a hallway. You may have to practise recall of these less definitive mnemonics a few times more than usual, but it is good practice to spend some time recalling any mnemonics that you're going to need.

25
LINKING 1

Can you recall what I asked you to remember last time?

Holmes finished his little lecture, and raised an eyebrow. “I trust that you grasp the principle of linking memories together, my dear Watson.”

“Of course,” I said, a little stiffly.

“Capital. The key to bedding the list down in your memory is, as before, recalling it. So when you practise the list, start with the mnemonic for the first item and progress down the list. If you falter or hesitate, stop, and refresh yourself briefly on the item that defied you. Then start again, from the beginning. Repeat as necessary until you can produce the whole list correctly, in sequence. You may then consider that as one successful recall.”

I nodded.

“I know it sounds like hard work, and it is, but each mnemonic you memorise makes the next easier, and each linked chain you commit makes the next bed down more swiftly and securely. Like any clever worker, the brain goes to great lengths to reduce the effort involved in tasks that it knows will be repeated. For now, recall the entire list three or four times immediately, a couple more times in fifteen minutes, then again in an hour, in four hours, in the evening, tomorrow a couple of times, and so on. Space out the recalls in increasing intervals, but keep performing them, and that will show the brain that you will need the information available for an indefinite period. In time, you find the mere act of making the chain of mnemonics engraves the list permanently, but you absolutely must patiently train your mind to treat these matters seriously. You would not expect to be a master marksman upon first picking up a rifle.”

“I understand, old chap,” I assured him. “Practice, practice, practice.”

“Exactly! So here’s a brief list of items of menswear to memorise: a top hat, a jacket, a bow tie, gloves and a pair of calf-high boots.”

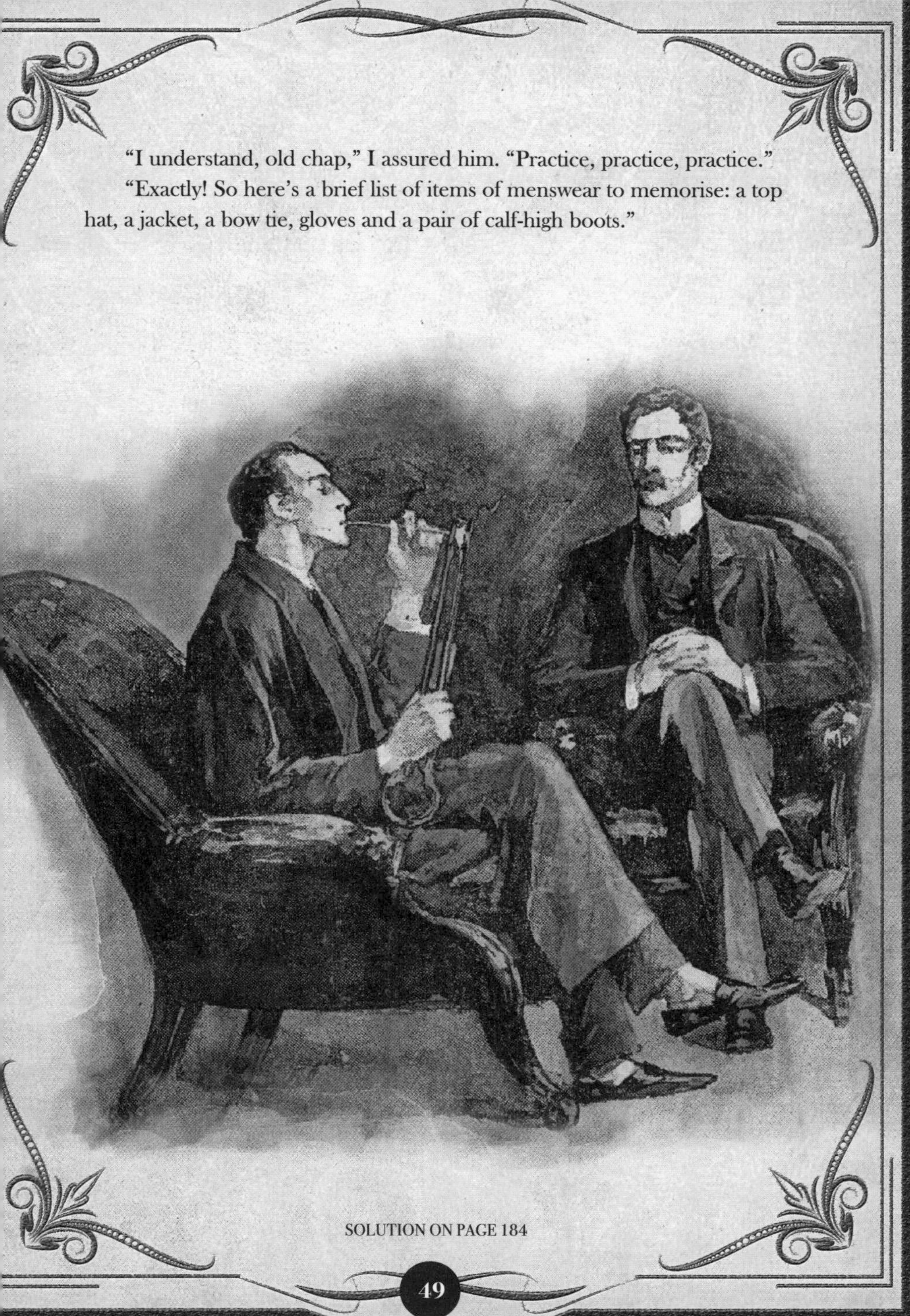

SOLUTION ON PAGE 184

THE LURCHER

We had Wiggins and his Irregulars observing the movements of one Henry Grey, originally of Basildon but lately engaged in assorted criminal activities around Forest Hill. Holmes suspected that he was in cahoots with the Alderman whose fish I have alluded to before.

When Wiggins returned to report, he sounded bemused. "Your bloke is pretending to walk funny, Mister Holmes," he said.

"Oh?" Sherlock looked entirely unsurprised by this information.

"Yeah. We trailed him all the way up Wimpole Street and Devonshire Place, and he was walking awfully peculiar – all exaggerated and careful, alternating long and short steps, with never a mind to everyone gawking at him as he passed. Then he dropped it entirely to cross Marylebone Road, then went back to being odd along the road and up York Gate, all hop, hop, twitch, hop. When he got into Regent's Park, he lost all pretence of any strangeness in his gait, and ambled around as freely as a bird. Like you thought, he eventually went into St Mark's."

"Excellent work, Wiggins," Holmes said, and passed over some coins. "I'm sure the good doctor here can clear up Grey's walking pattern for you."

Once Wiggins had departed, Holmes made it clear that I had grossly over-thought the matter.

Can you see the reason for Grey's oddities?

SOLUTION ON PAGE 184

CLIVE & Co

TRIO

I was wrestling with *The Times*, trying to get a potentially interesting article to a convenient size, when Holmes pulled me up with a sharply-barked, "Watson!"

I paused, and looked up at him. "Whatever is it, old chap?"

"Imagine three chaps in a row for me."

That made me blink, but I did as I was bidden, and laid the mess of newsprint in my lap. "Very well, Holmes."

"I will tell you that you can find Arthur positioned somewhere to the left of Barry. Similarly, Colin is somewhere in the line to the right of Arthur. Can you inform me of any of those three worthies' positions in the row with any certainty?"

What do you think?

SOLUTION ON PAGE 184

DARKNESS

Holmes and I were on Gray's Inn Road one evening so that my dear friend could examine the premises of a particular flour merchant. He had some suspicions that the merchant might be the source of a distinctive grain blend that he suspected of being key in the Spitstone Bakery Affair. So far as I could tell, our efforts had proven fruitless.

Out of the blue, he turned to me and asked, "Have you experienced a solar eclipse, Watson?"

"No," I told him. "I gather it is quite the experience."

"Yes, it is most singular. Uncomfortable for most people – and animals, for that matter. But given that they occur when the Moon obscures the Sun, and the Moon orbits the Earth approximately every four weeks, why are they not monthly affairs?"

Do you know the answer?

SOLUTION ON PAGE 185

CULPEPPER

The Culpepper murder was all the talk of the town, for a few days. The old man had been unpopular but well-known and wealthy, which made for a lot of public interest in the matter of his death. Lestrade was put under quite an amount of pressure, and inevitably he turned to Holmes for assistance.

The crux of his problem was that he had three primary suspects, members of a group of odd jobs men operating out of Battersea. All three had worked on Culpepper's house in the weeks prior to the murder, and they all lacked meaningful alibis. Unfortunately for the Inspector, they were a clannish and close-mouthed group, and he'd had great difficulty in getting any of them to say anything at all. He was of high opinion of the group's character as a whole, insisting that it had to be just one singular rotten element who had done the deed, and that the remainder were honest and hard-working.

From the three men, he had obtained precisely two informative statements. The first insisted that the second had not killed anyone, and the second insisted that the third had not done so either. The third, apparently, would not so much as speak his name to the Inspector.

Holmes put it to me this way: assuming the Inspector's certainty about their characters to be correct – that is, the murderer must necessarily be lying, and the innocent men must be telling the truth...

Who was the murderer?

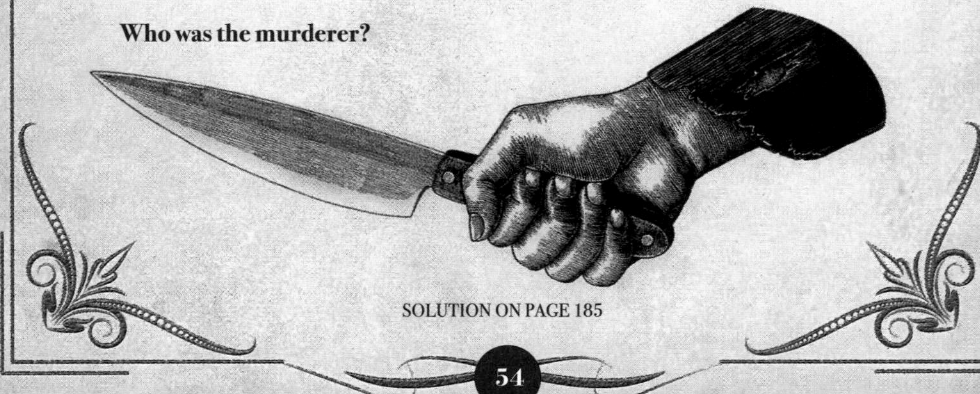

SOLUTION ON PAGE 185

30

SHIPSHAPE

I had just finished with a plate of Mrs Hudson's kippers in parsley sauce when Holmes waggled a sensationalist journal in my direction. "Here's a little something for you," he said.

"Please, do tell," I replied. I was grateful that I'd been permitted the chance to finish my repast.

"This is an amusing report from Hobart, in Tasmania. Some decades ago, a pair of truculent captains got in a disagreement over whose ship was faster, and entered into a wager. They would race around the globe, one heading East and one heading West, and see who returned first."

I could see which way the wind was blowing, so to speak. "Ah," I said.

"Quite, Watson. The two returned, some weeks later, appearing on the horizon at the same time."

"Did they?" I asked.

"It says so right here, old chap. Surely you wouldn't doubt *The Gentleman's Informer.*"

"Perish the thought."

"Well, then. The two docked, and were about to call the whole wager off when they discovered they disagreed on the correct date by two whole days. Why do you imagine that was?"

Do you know the answer?

SOLUTION ON PAGE 185

SECTION TWO

MEDIUM

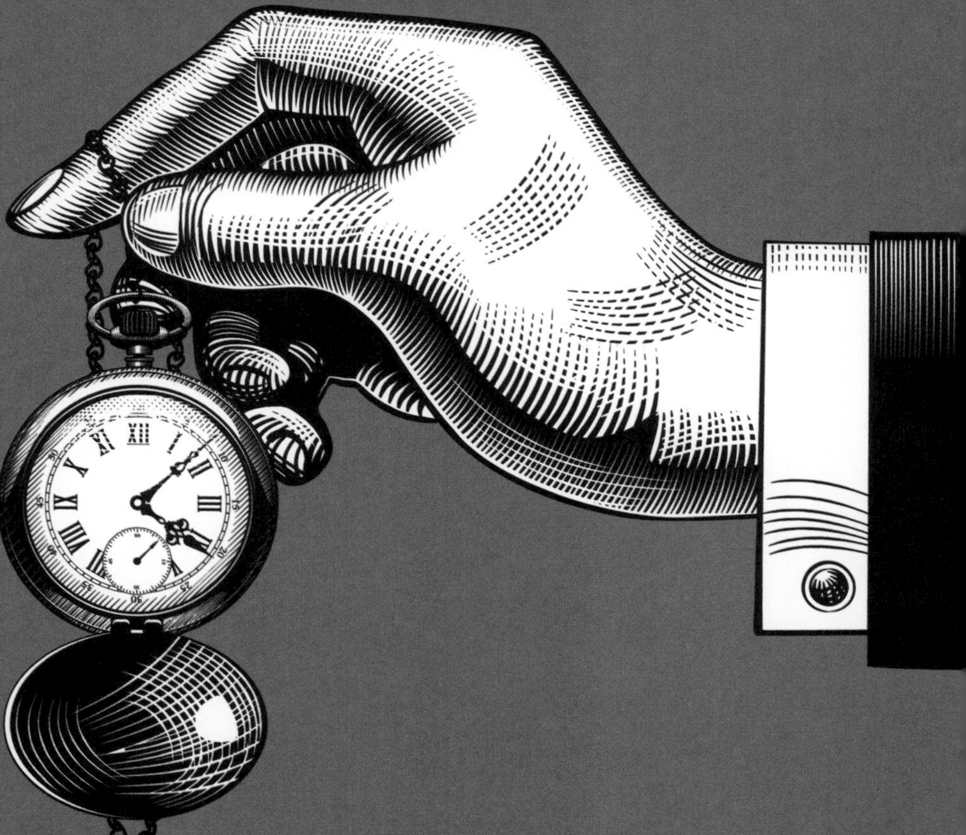

31
LINKING 2

On previous occasions, when testing my recall of a mnemonic image, Holmes had taken pains to check my memory of the image before presenting me with a new item to memorise. Not so on this occasion.

"It is perfectly simple to memorise multiple linked chains, my dear Watson. Indeed, the technique would hardly be worth mentioning if it were only possible to retain one. So, with that in mind, I would like you to make a chain of some new items and practise recalling it at least a couple of times before we test your previous chain. I'm aware that merely saying this will tend to make the first chain come to mind, but so it goes."

I nodded amiably, and put the first chain from my thoughts for a moment.

"Capital. For this second chain, let's turn to foodstuffs. A jar of honey, an apple, two fried eggs, a cucumber, a loaf of bread and a cup of piping hot tea."

I set to work constructing alternately absurd and fiendish mnemonics, and once I'd linked everything thoroughly, I ran through the list verbally a few times.

"Good," Holmes said. "Now, what were the items in the first linked chain?"

It took me a worried moment, but once I had my initial mnemonic for the chain, I had them all. Can you do it?

SOLUTION ON PAGE 186

32

RULE

"Watson, come here."

I looked up. Holmes was standing by one of the side tables, looking expectant. I duly rose to my feet and crossed the room. "Yes, old chap?"

He pointed to the table, on which were arranged four plain cards, each bearing a single handwritten character, thus:

A	B
1	2

"Observe these cards," he said. "Ah, no touching."

I nodded, and withdrew my hand.

"Each card bears a letter on one side, and a number on the other. This is a fact. Now let me tell you a rule. If a card has a vowel on one side, then it has an odd number on the other side."

"Very well," I said.

"My question is, which cards do you need to turn over to ascertain whether any of the cards break the rule?"

SOLUTION ON PAGE 186

FÖHN

Holmes was making his way through one of his sensationalist crime magazines when he announced, apropos of nothing, "It's an ill wind, they say."

"That blows no good?" I asked.

He looked up at me. "What? No. The Föhn."

"Ah," I said. "Of course. Foolish of me."

"It's a hot, strong, dry wind that gusts down from the mountains under certain conditions. The superstitious say that it can drive men mad, lead them to despair or devilry. I can attest that it is reasonably unpleasant to be in."

"I see."

"Do you? Tell me then, how is it that a wind coming down off a snow-laden mountain can be hot and dry?"

SOLUTION ON PAGE 186

34

GARLIC NUTS

Mrs Hudson is an excellent person, but she does have a lamentable tendency to experiment with her biscuit selections. I am not an unadventurous man, but I do draw the line at tampering with ginger nuts. The substitution of garlic for ginger produces a deeply unpleasant result.

I was eyeing the biscuit plate cautiously one morning when Holmes clapped me on the shoulder. "This is a salutary moment, Watson," he told me.

"Really," I replied.

"But of course. We must never turn aside from a chance at improving your mind, old chap."

The penny dropped. "Ah."

"Take one hundred ginger nuts, precisely one half of them made with the garlic recipe you so despise. You have the two types separated, and two large jars. Your task is to place all of the biscuits into the two jars in any way that you see fit. Afterwards, you will be blindfolded, and one biscuit for you to consume will be selected at random from one of the jars, also selected randomly."

"That seems somewhat Byzantine," I said.

Holmes quirked an eyebrow. "Even so."

"How would you arrange the biscuits to give yourself the best odds of getting a pleasant ginger nut, and what are those odds?"

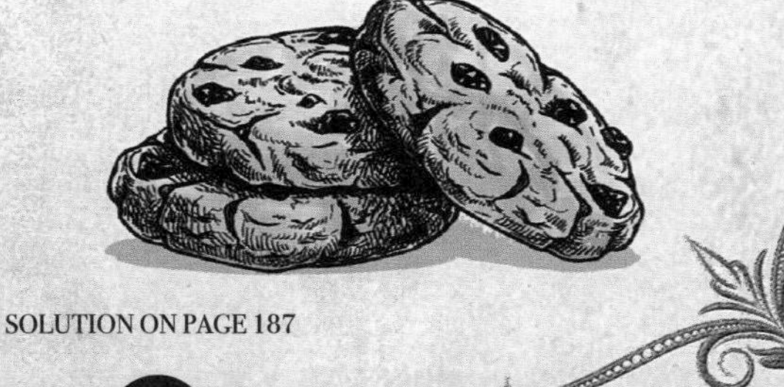

SOLUTION ON PAGE 187

LIARS

"Indulge me a moment," Holmes said to me one morning.

I put down my teacup. "Always, my dear fellow."

"Please, conjure up three worthies of dubious reliability. Those fellows we encountered in the Lazarus Ales Brewery stockroom seem eminent candidates. Their names, if you recall, were Ted, Adam and Matthew."

I most certainly did not recall, but I did retain a vague mental image of the trio. They had proven spectacularly unhelpful during the Spitstone Bakery Affair. I obediently called them to mind. "I am ready," I said.

"So. We have one statement from each of the three men. Ted attests that Adam is a liar. Adam claims that Matthew is a liar. Matthew, in turn, insists that both Ted and Adam are liars. We do not know the honesty of the three, except that each person's claim definitely applies to the statements we have. However, the three are correctly aware of the accuracy of each other's statements."

"Perhaps I overstated my readiness, old chap."

"Nevertheless, please tell me who, if anyone, is telling us the truth, assuming that said truth is logically consistent?"

SOLUTION ON PAGE 187

36

MOST FOUL

I was reading when Holmes waved one of his crime periodicals at me, distracting me from the day's news of imperial affairs on the subcontinent.

"Yes, old chap?"

He favoured me with a tight, fleeting smile. "There's an interesting case in here that you might usefully consider. An Epping man, one Richard Wilkins, was recently accused of murdering a rival. The prosecution's case involved his possession of a blackjack. Wilkins had given a statement that he had indeed had the blackjack on his person at the time of the murder, in the outside left-hand pocket of his coat, but insisted he had been carrying it solely for personal protection. In fact, he maintained that the cosh remained completely untouched between his leaving home that morning and being arrested by the police."

"I see," I said.

"The arresting officer's report clearly stated that the blackjack had been found within the inside right-hand pocket of Wilkins's coat. The prosecutor maintained that this proved Wilkins as a liar, and was strong evidence of the blackjack having seen use – specifically, on the victim. As it transpired, however, the defendant had been perfectly honest, both about the blackjack and about his innocence."

Can you explain?

SOLUTION ON PAGE 187

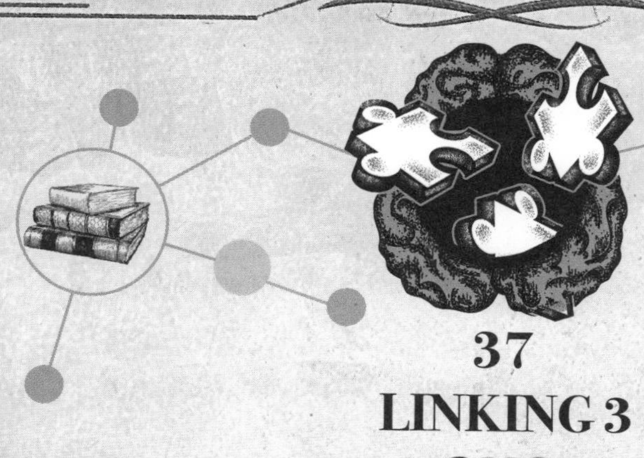

37
LINKING 3

I was busy tamping down my pipe when Holmes announced that he had another list of objects for me to memorise. "Once again, set aside the previous lists for the moment. I want you to make a new linked chain of mnemonic images, and practise them a few times."

I nodded, and settled myself to pay attention.

Holmes looked at my hand. "On this occasion, perhaps we will try a list of needful things – a pipe, a newspaper, a book, a grandfather clock, a magnifying glass, a medical syringe and box of matches."

I withheld comment on Holmes's ideas of what might be generally needful, and set myself to constructing suitably bizarre images to link the ideas together. Once I had them all developed, I ran through several practises of recalling the list, and announced this fact.

"Good, Watson," Holmes said. "Now, what was the previous list of items I asked you to remember?"

Do you remember?

SOLUTION ON PAGE 188

ROULETTE

The Case of the Bewildering Banker took us to several unlikely places, one such being a rather upscale London casino that had been in operation since the late 1820s. We were there to observe a pair of the Banker's associates, whom I had privately labelled "Top Hat" and "Monocle" for reasons that I am quite certain you can deduce.

We had observed the two men in conversation beforehand, but they took pains to enter the casino separately. They made their way to the same roulette table, but sat quite far apart, and studiously ignored each other. They restricted themselves entirely to outside bets, and invariably picked opposing spreads. When Top Hat bet on red, Monocle covered black. If Monocle went Low, Top Hat would pick High.

Most spins, one or the other won, precisely recouping the loss that the other had made, but every so often, zero would land and both would lose. The croupier noticed almost immediately, of course, but ignored the matter.

After a while, we left, and I asked Holmes about the croupier's disinterest.

"That's elementary, my dear Watson. All manner of fools convince themselves that they can beat the roulette table, and develop complex systems for that purpose, but of course they cannot. The zero spot ensures that the casino will always win. The croupier is under orders to let them try as they like."

"So all that Top Hat and Monocle were doing was slowly losing money?"

"Not at all. Do try to pay attention, Watson. They were not attempting to operate a poorly thought-out gambling system. Their process was highly effective."

What were they doing?

SOLUTION ON PAGE 188

39

TRANSPARENT

"Here's a little something for your mind to chew on, Watson."

This seemingly random sally on Holmes's part came as I was looking out of the window at the comings and goings on Baker Street. It was a foul day, and consequently the few people out in the weather were scurrying around quite frantically, the poor devils.

"Oh?" I kept my voice mild.

"Tell me, which common material becomes less transparent when you wipe it with a perfectly clean, dry cloth? You may assume that the cloth does not leave any fibres behind."

It took me quite a bit of mental "chewing" to find the solution.

Can you think of an answer?

SOLUTION ON PAGE 188

40

COLD SNAP

One chilly morning, Holmes and I were making our way back along Baker Street to 221b. Seeing a light dusting of snow settled on window ledges and other opportune surfaces, I made some comment or other about the season getting cooler.

Holmes, naturally, leapt on it as an opportunity to engage my brain. "Ah, yes, the cold. You will note, my dear Watson, that it is somewhat above freezing, and yet there is some snow visible around us. And I assume you have heard the common phrase 'too cold for snow' regarding cold weather."

"Yes," I said, intending it to serve for both his points.

"Have you given thought to it being too cold for snow?"

"Ah–"

He kept on going.

"Are the frozen poles not extremely snowy, and yet also extremely cold? If the phrase is wrong, why has it retained common usage? What's behind all this?"

SOLUTION ON PAGE 189

41

FALLS

"Have you ever heard a man fall to his death from a high cliff?"

I put down my piece of toast and turned to give Holmes a look of utter perplexity. "No, thanks be to God. Have you?"

"Indeed," he said dryly. "Have you at least imagined hearing such a thing?"

"No!"

"Then try it now." His face was set in that firm, insistent expression I have come to associate with his little tests and self-improvements.

I nodded. "Very well." I did so. It was ghastly.

"Well, man? What did you hear?"

"A horrible scream fading away into the distance, followed by a nastily wet thud."

"Wrong, Watson. Try again."

Why did Holmes say my description was wrong?

SOLUTION ON PAGE 189

42

ONE APPLE

I was reading the newspaper early one afternoon when Holmes plucked an apple from the fruit bowl and tossed it at me. After a moment's panic, I managed to use the paper to catch it.

"Thank you?" I said.

"An apple a day... But tell me, Doctor. Have you heard of recurring decimal numbers?"

I eyed him warily. "Yes? 0.111... and so on? Schoolboy stuff, old chap."

"Well then, would you say that 0.99... recurring is less than 1?"

"Yes, plainly," I said.

"Oh? Tell me then, how much less is it?"

SOLUTION ON PAGE 189

Loci

After I'd spent a week or two working on chained lists, Holmes explained that while that method was good, there was a better option. I wasn't delighted to hear that, in truth, but his explanation did make sense.

Don't fret so, Watson. You had to practise combining mnemonics together, and chaining is still a very potent option. It is simply that the technique of loci is better. It means "Places" in Latin, and the singular is locus. Humans are strongly adapted to memorise familiar environments. It's vital, in the wild, to be able to get back to your camp when you need to. So we remember familiar routes. Everyone's facility is different here of course, but I'll touch on that later.

To start off, I want you to think of a stretch of route that you know well, one that you have walked so frequently that you could almost do it with your eyes closed. For example, the path from your childhood bedroom to the garden gate outside, or maybe a clockwise loop around these apartments, starting from the front door and keeping the wall at your left hand.

I'd like you to bring such a route to mind now.

You have one? Good. The next step is to think of notable places and de facto landmarks along the route. This will break the route into stages, and every time you walk the route in your mind, the stages will occur in the same order. It may help you to write the stages and their landmarks out, in longhand, on a piece of paper, because the memory has no particular reason to consider your route in those terms unless you encourage it.

The goal of this is to come up with an ordered set of images which you can then combine with items to create a memorised list. People who have very little sense of direction or difficulty recalling spatial routes do have options here. One could use lyrics from well-known music and pick vivid words, for example, or perhaps use the physical stages involved in a very familiar mechanical task of some sort, such as cleaning a fireplace.

These loci form the foundational corridors of the palaces of memory to which I commit my knowledge of crime and its related fields.

They are more vivid than a simple chain of mnemonics, easier to memorise, and less prone to breaking – for, if one forgets one item in the list, one still has the next locus on the route to bring the next item to mind. For a simple chain, a slip like that means not being able to continue. Also, as one uses the loci, it gets easier to know them by relative position, so if you need to recall the ninth item along your path, you do not have to recall the previous eight, because you can leap to the appropriate locus.

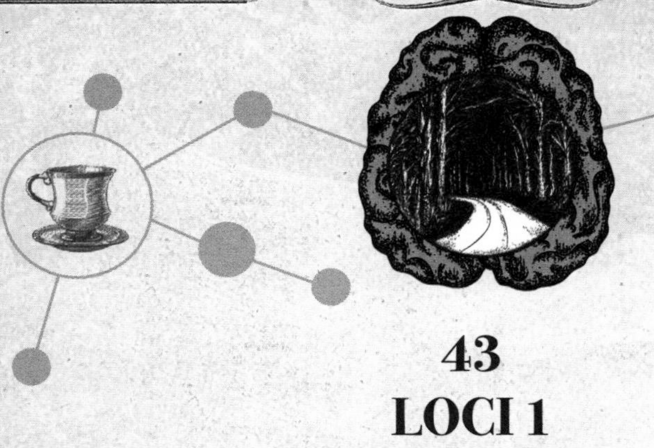

43
LOCI 1

When I pondered physical routes that I remembered well, the one that leapt to my mind was the route to my first surgery. From the Metropolitan Railway stop, there was a pleasant six-minute walk to the surgery itself. Then I invariably went through the door in the tall wood-planked fence wall, through the courtyard, into the building, past the receptionist's desk and the door to the nurse's office, up the stairs, along a short corridor, into my office and, finally, to my desk. To my surprise, remembering it was almost as vivid as walking it in reality. There were fifteen clear stages along the whole route.

"I see you are looking into the past, Watson," Holmes said. "Capital, my dear fellow. I would like you to now enhance the points on your route, to make them stronger in your mind. The way to do this is to add other sensory elaborations. In an ideal world, one would take the time to associate unique and plausibly-related sounds, scents, textures, colours, even tastes to each of the loci along your chosen route. Routes can be reused in various ways, so do not fear that this is all for a one-off utility."

"Even so, that sounds like a lot of work."

"Quite. These elaborations need to be chained into your memory of each stage's landmark, and practice is required. Writing the elaborations for each stage out first helps initially, when one is most uncertain. With sufficient effort, it can become automatic to associate, say, that table with the scent of roses and the humming of a bee. But I am not an unreasonable man."

I nodded non-committally.

"For now, I would like you to ensure that your route has at least ten stages, and then I would like you to add one unique sensory impression to each landmark. You should know by now that for the best results, you are to practise frequent recollection of the entire route with increasing amounts of time between each practice."

I nodded again.

"By the way. What was the third linked chain of items I asked you to memorise?"

Can you remember?

SOLUTION ON PAGE 190

TERMINUS

One afternoon, Holmes read an entry in one of his crime periodicals to me. He then challenged me to explain the circumstances.

The gist of it was that a Chigwell-based bank teller in his late fifties was murdered one evening in his house. He and his wife lived there alone, their children having long since moved out, and were widely considered to be a very happy couple.

According to the wife, she had been preparing supper when she heard conversation in her husband's study. Investigating, she discovered that the door was locked. Her husband let out a yell of protest, and then fell silent. She was unable to get any further response, so went round to the study window, which was open, unusual given the season. She pulled the curtain aside, and saw her husband lying dead with a dagger in his chest. No-one had visited the house, and she insisted that anyone trying to sneak in and out would have found it very difficult given that the study window was at the front of the house and readily visible to all and sundry.

Police reports verified the physical details suggested by the wife's story. The intruder had left no clear sign of his presence, and his motive in slaying a seemingly innocuous banker baffled them entirely. Their investigations into his movements ruled out the possibility that he had somehow learned of information so sensitive it was worth killing him for. His place of work was not robbed or defrauded over the following months. The wife was quickly discounted as a suspect on account of her arthritis, significant enough in her hands to make stabbing her husband through the heart quite impossible. There were no enemies or rivals, no paramour on either side, no criminals or colleagues to benefit by the man's absence, and no suddenly-enriched relatives – the will left his entire estate to his wife.

Holmes seemed to find the matter almost insultingly trivial, so I was not delighted when I had to struggle to find an answer.

What do you think?

SOLUTION ON PAGE 190

SOLAR

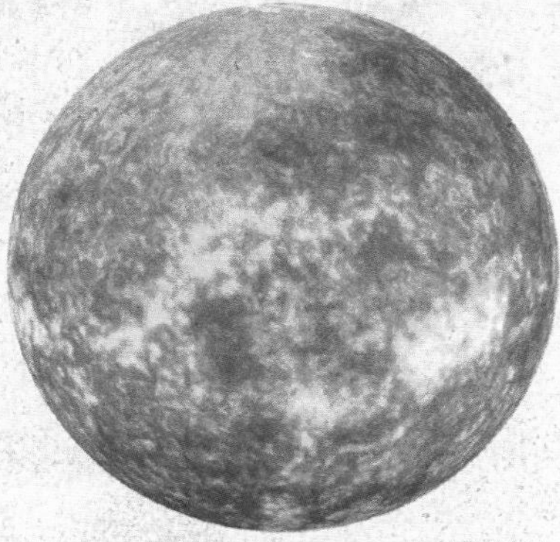

"Have you thought about orbits, Watson?"

I glanced at Holmes curiously. "I didn't know you had even the first interest in astronomy, old chap."

He shrugged eloquently. "It is of supreme irrelevance to the problem of the criminal mind, it's true. But it does offer a number of useful opportunities to spur on the development of your mental faculties. Besides, there are very few topics regarding which I am not at least slightly curious, if weightier matters do not claim me."

"I see," I said. "Well, I must admit that I have not given the matter much detailed thought. The Earth orbits the Sun, the Moon orbits the Earth, and so on."

"Precisely. But the Sun is much, much larger than the Earth. Why does the Sun not pull the Moon away from us?"

"Well..." I began. Then I had to close my mouth and think about it for a while.

What do you reckon?

SOLUTION ON PAGE 191

TONE

Eventually, the Spitstone Bakery Affair dragged Holmes and I out to the south-west coast, to the Hookland so beloved of Nolan and Southwell. It's an odd little county, and large swathes of it are still surprisingly pastoral. Charming though, in its own peculiar way, and well worth searching out.

As we were approaching our destination, in a cart nonetheless, we passed a fellow hammering a thick pole into the ground, not far from a clearly demarcated field. Holmes perked up a little at this, and after listening intently for a moment, drew my attention to a clear ringing tone that accompanied each blow of the sledgehammer.

"You will note," he said to me, "that the pole that chap is working on is wooden. So the impact of his blows is not the source of the ringing tone. Where do you imagine it is coming from?"

I had to confess that I could not identify its source.

Can you?

SOLUTION ON PAGE 191

47

SENTENCE

I was perusing that week's edition of the *British Medical Journal* one afternoon when Holmes looked up from some scurrilous newspaper or other with a glint in his eye.

"Here, Watson. This may prove instructive."

"More so than reports on Medical and Surgical Practice in the Hospitals and Asylums of the British Empire?" I asked mildly.

"Let us say differently so."

I put down the journal. "Very well."

"There's a report in this paper about the experience one Thomas Spare had in an Ottoman prison."

"I say!"

"Don't fear, old friend. I do not believe its veracity. Fortunately, that is moot. The report states that Spare was not plainly told the length of his sentence. Instead, he was informed that his prison guard was fifty-two years of age, and that his sentence would be completed when the man's age was twice his own – which, at the time, was twenty-four.

Waving aside technicalities like precise dates of birthdays, how old would this make Spare on his release?"

SOLUTION ON PAGE 192

48

TARGET

I was never a particularly good shot. Despite my time in the army, my interests always lay in putting people back together rather than breaking them apart, and so marksmanship was something I engaged with uneasily, at best. But in my time in the service, I did see some truly astonishing shots taken on the practice field. Given the right conditions, it is quite awe-inspiring how distant a target some men were able to hit.

I made some such comment to Holmes one day, and of course he leapt on it as an opportunity to engage my mind.

"I am sure you know about trajectory," he said to me. "Aiming up at an angle to increase distance, and so on."

I nodded.

"Did you also know that over very great distances, you also have to take the movement of the Earth into account?"

I dimly recalled some such thing. "Perhaps," I admitted.

"Tell me, then."

"If you were here, in London, shooting at a very distant target to your north, and had calculated your vertical deflection to ensure the correct trajectory, would you need to aim to the left of your target, or to the right?"

SOLUTION ON PAGE 192

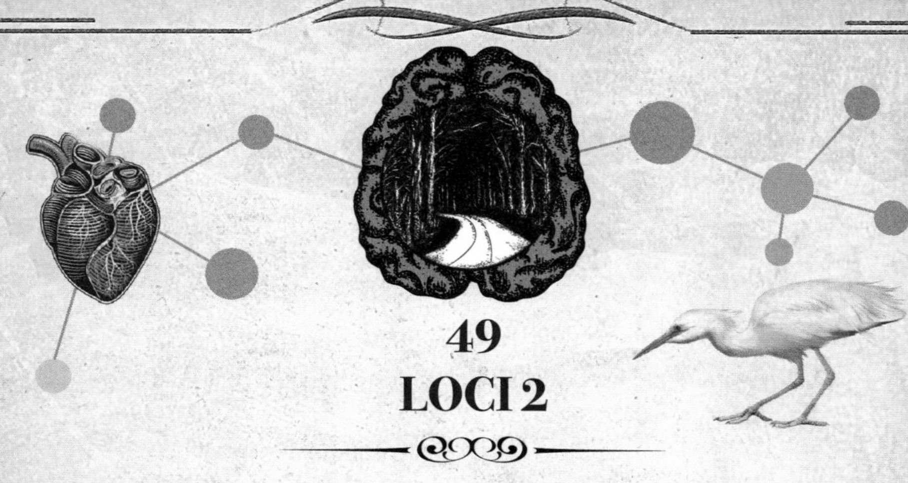

49
LOCI 2

In the days following Holmes's first discussion of loci, I did indeed manage to associate a sensory impression to each of the fifteen steps on my mental route from the train station to my old surgery desk. He repeatedly hinted that I might add a second or even a third extra sense to each location, but that I refrained from. Nevertheless, after more than a score of recollections over the course of a week, I had a fluent sense of the progression of the journey in my head.

I recounted my route's landmarks and their sensory associations to Holmes, at his prompting, and was rewarded with a nod of approval.

"Well done, Watson. Now let's put it to use, shall we? I will produce for you a list of ten items taken, I fancy, from the titles of comparatively recent novels. I would like you to use mnemonic imagery to associate the items in the list with the loci along your route, in order from the first. It can be worthwhile to include at least a little imagery leading from one mnemonic to the next, but your loci should be your primary means of recall. When practising the list, if you fail to remember one item, move on to the next, letting your route prompt you correctly, and only at the end refresh your memory and restart the recall anew. Needless to say, affecting the other sensory associations of your loci in your mnemonic is advantageous."

"I understand," I said.

"Excellent. Jot this list down, and get to work: a heart, five children, a white bird, a hotel, four feathers, the moon, a green shutter, a purple cloud, a boat and a brass bottle."

I thus charge you to attach the same list of concepts to your own route. You can recall it swiftly and smoothly, yes?

SOLUTION ON PAGE 193

50

NOTES

I was still in the process of waking up one morning when Holmes passed me a small wooden box. I took it from him automatically, and opened it to find a small stack of handwritten notes, each containing one short sentence.

Bemused, I leafed through them. They read as follows:

None of these statements are true.
Exactly one of these statements is true.
Exactly two of these statements are true.
Exactly three of these statements are true.
Exactly four of these statements are true.
Exactly five of these statements are true.
All of these statements are true.

"Good morning, Watson. Which, if any, of the notes in the box are true?"

SOLUTION ON PAGE 193

51

TWINKLER

During our investigations into the Culpepper Murder, Holmes and I spent several long evenings in Battersea Park waiting for skulduggery that never took place. Well, I say Holmes and I. Actually, after the second such evening, he graciously allowed that I might prefer to remain home. I am not ashamed to say that I took advantage of his generosity. I have little fondness for nocturnal mud.

On the second evening, which was cold and clear, he nodded up at the Moon, which was waxing gibbous. "Not exactly twinkling," he said conversationally.

"No," I agreed.

"Ah, but do you know why not, my dear Watson? The stars are."

Can you figure out the answer?

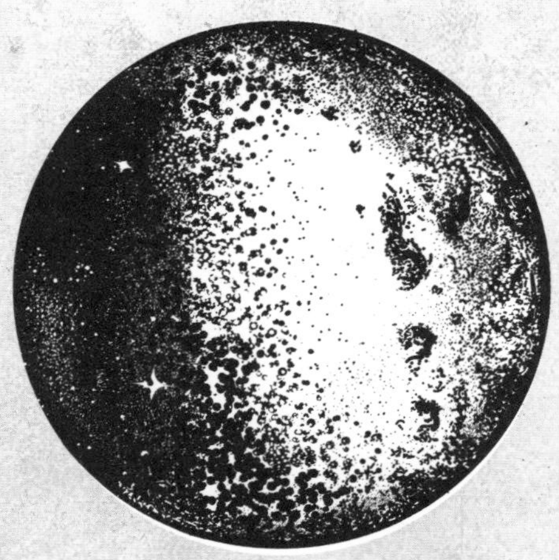

SOLUTION ON PAGE 194

BUBBLE

"You've seen a soap bubble, I assume." Holmes was toying an alembic thoughtfully and looking in my direction. From the smell, it was not anything related to soap that he was experimenting on.

"Indeed," I said. "Lovely things. I have chased many, in my day."

He nodded. "I suppose you would have, at that. Tell me, then. Would you think that the pressure of the air inside a soap bubble is less than, equal to, or greater than the pressure of the air outside it?"

I stifled the temptation to suggest that I would not generally think about the pressure of air inside a soap bubble at all, and sought a satisfactory response.

Do you know the correct answer?

SOLUTION ON PAGE 194

53

CANE

On the Case of the Alderman's Trout, Holmes and I ended up searching a rather seedy little tenement building in Camden Town. The area has moments of charm, but not enough to make it a desirable destination. Still, there we were.

While sifting through the jumbled detritus of our suspect's hurried departure, we came across a large number of pieces of cane. After a period of examination, Holmes announced that the canes had originally been four feet in length, and that they had all been clumsily broken, more or less at random.

Then he straightened, and turned to me. "Imagine, Watson, that these canes had actually been divided into two parts randomly. On average, how much longer would the longer portion be than the shorter portion?"

He caught me off guard. "How can I possibly answer that?" I demanded.

"Really, Watson. It is quite elementary."

I stifled a sigh, and did my best to think about it carefully.

Can you see the answer?

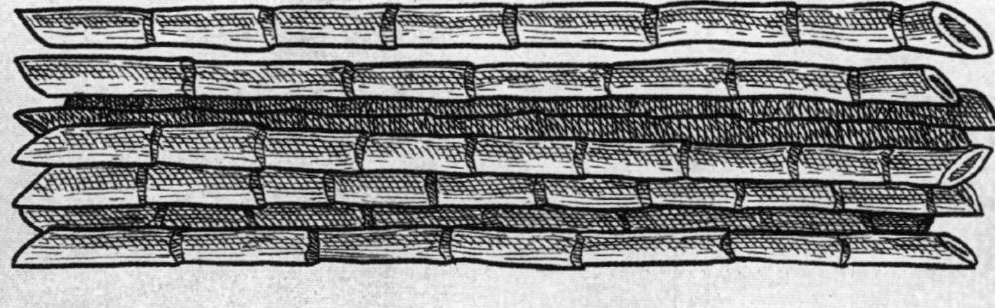

SOLUTION ON PAGE 195

54

CULPABILITY

Having made rather a fool of himself with his previous pool of suspects, Lestrade was a little more circumspect in his next approach to Holmes in the matter of the Culpepper Murder. After a significant amount of detailed police work – asking questions and checking documents, that is – the Inspector decided that he had been right about the Battersea odd-job men as a whole. He had merely not selected the correct individuals. So he had rounded up three more, and he was certain this time that one of the three was the murderer.

As before, Lestrade insisted that the honesty of the innocent individuals could be relied upon as absolutely as the dishonesty of the guilty one. The statements from this second trio were as taciturn as those of the first group had been. The first man said only that the second man was innocent. The second said that the third man was guilty. The third said nothing whatsoever.

Assuming Lestrade to be correct in his assumptions, which of them, if any, was actually guilty?

SOLUTION ON PAGE 195

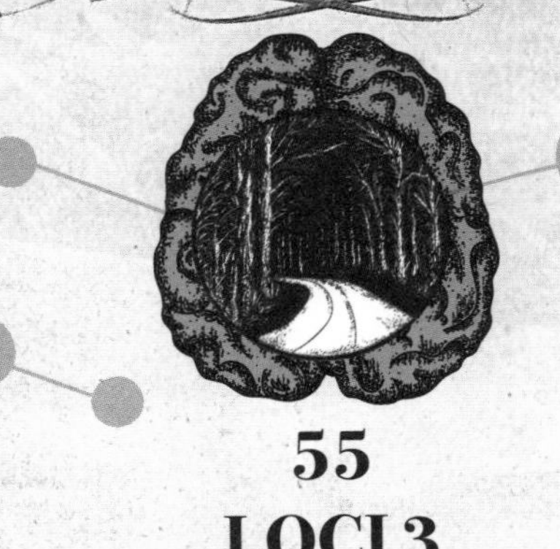

55
LOCI 3

During a quiet moment some days after presenting me with the previous list of items to attach to my route, Holmes continued his discussion on the use of these loci.

"I told you that your route would not be a single-use thing, my dear Watson. I did not deceive you. Even so, I would encourage you to prepare a number of routes for use, in order to maximise the versatility of your memory. It is just good practice to assemble a number of different environments to hang mnemonics off."

That seemed broadly reasonable, if potentially unnecessary in my case. "How many do you have, old chap?"

He looked amused. "Currently? Seventeen thousand, eight hundred and twenty three."

I stared at him.

"I am a quite unusual case," he said blandly. "If you need to reuse a route, time is one option. Give it no thought at all for about twice as long as you spent practising recall of it from first instance through to most recent, and it will start to fade. Again, we are all different, but time will wipe it for you."

"It's not permanent?"

"So long as you keep up occasionally recalling it, your mind will keep it available. When you turn away from it deliberately, your mind will decide it is less important."

"I see."

"The other option is more proactive. Go through your route, and

SOLUTION ON PAGE 196

cleanse each landmark with a torrent of fire, burning away every extraneous detail. Once it is burned clean, banish any marks or damage, and place a small, featureless white ball at the landmark. Your mind will pick up on your intent, and downplay the association. Again, you will need to practise this cleansing a few times. But it is far faster. Later, I will share better options with you, but for now, this is the one to practise."

I nodded.

"But first, please tell me my previous list of items."

Do you remember the previous list?

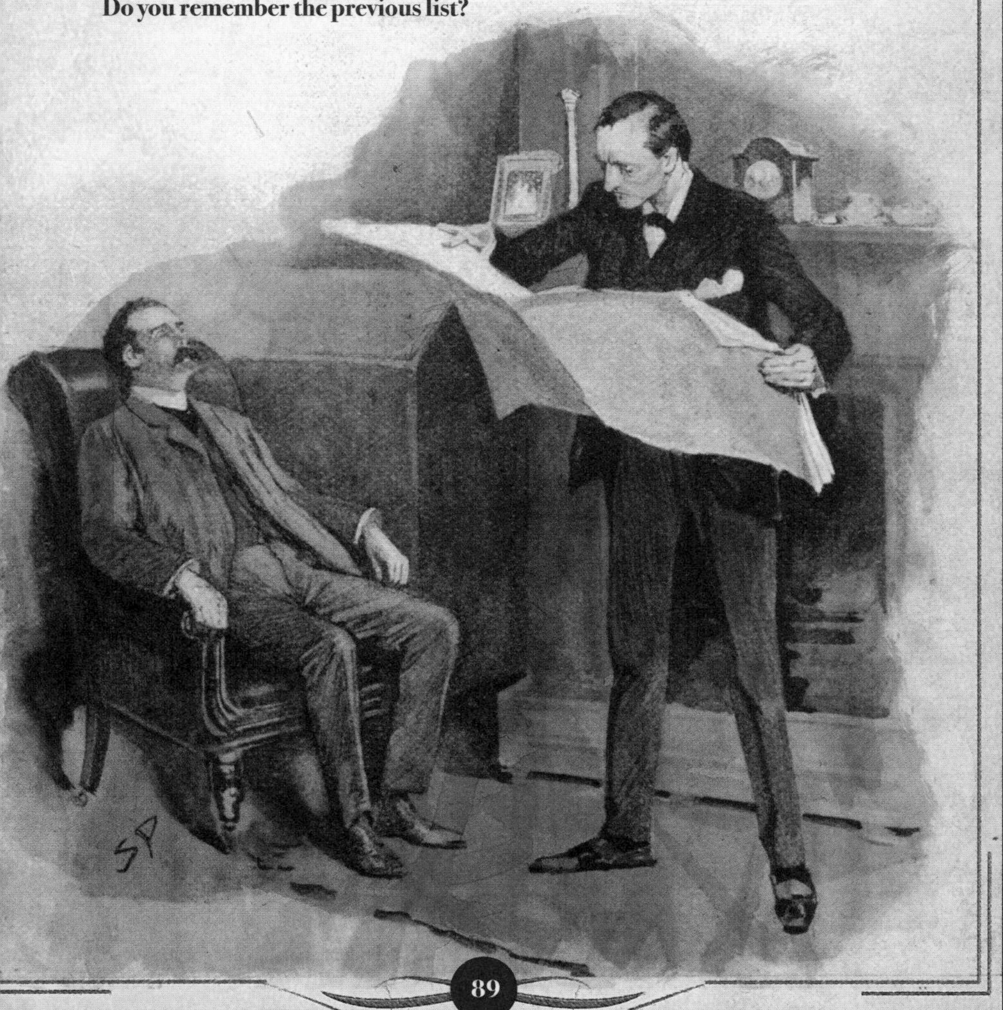

56

TRUEL

Holmes presented me with this somewhat peculiar question after he'd been at his lurid crime periodicals again. It was a Friday evening, coming at the end of a reasonably enjoyable week, but I did not stop to take notice of other details at the time, being pleasantly engaged with the work of Mr Jerome K. Jerome.

"Here's a enlivener for you, Watson," Holmes declared.

I looked up.

"Picture, if you will, three fellows engaged in a triangular pistol duel to the last man standing. In the interests of fairness, they are to take their shots starting with the man with the worst aim, then the medium shot, then the best marksman of the three, and continuing in this pattern until one survives. For the sake of mathematical precision, let us say that Worst will hit once in three shots, Medium will hit once in two, and Good will hit every time."

I tried to wrench my mind from three men in a boat to three men in a fight to the death, with only partial success. "Very well," I managed.

"If you assume that each man will adopt his best strategy, who should Worst open by shooting at?"

It took me a while to satisfy Holmes on the matter.

Can you deduce the solution?

SOLUTION ON PAGE 196

57

SALARY

We were crossing Tottenham Court Road one afternoon, having spent several hours in the company of a nervous but determined young woman whose fiancé worked on Fleet Street. A newspaper board with a headline about managerial pay caught Holmes's eye.

"The culture of secrecy regarding pay is a very foolish one," he declared. "It serves company owners and shareholders only, aiding them in the basest inequity. Honestly, Watson, the common man has no idea how much influence he would have at his fingertips, if only he could trust his fellows. But that is not how the mind works."

"Quite," I said, at a loss for any other answer.

"I recall a situation where a small group of Lloyds actuaries of my acquaintance – three of them – decided to calculate their average salary without any of them permitting his actual earnings to be calculable to the others. The lengths men go to... Still. How do you imagine they went about it?"

We were crossing Euston Road before I finally found a solution.

Can you figure out how they managed it?

SOLUTION ON PAGE 197

58

RECOLLECT

"Indulge me would you, my dear Watson?"

I looked over at him, seated pensively in his chair. "Of course, dear fellow. In what?"

"A recollection."

"Of course," I said.

"I was there, years ago now, when the Pendragon's Seat was destroyed. I remember the time quite clearly, one thirty-two in the morning. Mycroft had dispatched me to Winchester on an associated matter. How the chair had come to be there is a mystery for another time, and its links to King Arthur's period were tenuous at best, but it was a highly valuable relic. The fool who shattered it had no need to do so whatsoever. I think he did it in malice, lashing out in the moment of his own passing, determined to take something with him. It was an instructive moment for me, and I think about it often. Pettiness, Watson, is a force to never be underestimated. Men will drive themselves blithely to destruction out of vindictive spite, with no thought to the propriety of the target of their ire. If it were otherwise, I would hardly be needed here. The weather only underpinned the whole mess – it was wretched, all driving rain and heavy, bitingly cold wind." He fell broodingly silent.

"It sounds ghastly," I offered.

He nodded. "You've visited Winchester. Tell me, old friend. Could it have been possible that just twenty four hours after the event, it was bright and sunny?"

What do you think?

SOLUTION ON PAGE 197

59

CRIME

We were strolling across Hyde Park one lunchtime when Holmes said to me, apropos of nothing, "The law can undoubtedly be an ass, Watson."

"Quite," I said, wondering if we were technically breaking some obscure statute by not keeping to the left-hand side of the footpath, or failing to carry seed for the pigeons, or some such.

"There's a criminal act, under English law, that is harshly punishable if attempted unsuccessfully, but isn't prosecutable if undertaken successfully."

"How curious," I said.

"Do you know what it is?"

His tone made it clear that he expected me to find the answer.

Do you have any idea?

SOLUTION ON PAGE 197

CENTURY

Holmes and I were lingering over the breakfast table. Mrs Hudson had outdone herself – her bacon was quite something – and we were dawdling over our tea and newspapers.

"Do you know the century game, Watson?" asked Holmes.

I had to confess that I did not.

"It is a two-player affair, common amongst inmates of Wandsworth Prison."

"Perhaps it is not surprising that I don't know it," I said.

"Perhaps. The men take turns to state a number between 1 and 10, keeping count of the running total. The loser is the first man to reach or exceed 100. There is in fact a strategy for one of the two, either the one who goes first or the one who goes second, that will ensure victory every time. Can you deduce it? The enduring popularity of the game is not a testament to the inmates' arithmetical prowess."

What do you think?

SOLUTION ON PAGE 197

SECTION THREE
TRICKY

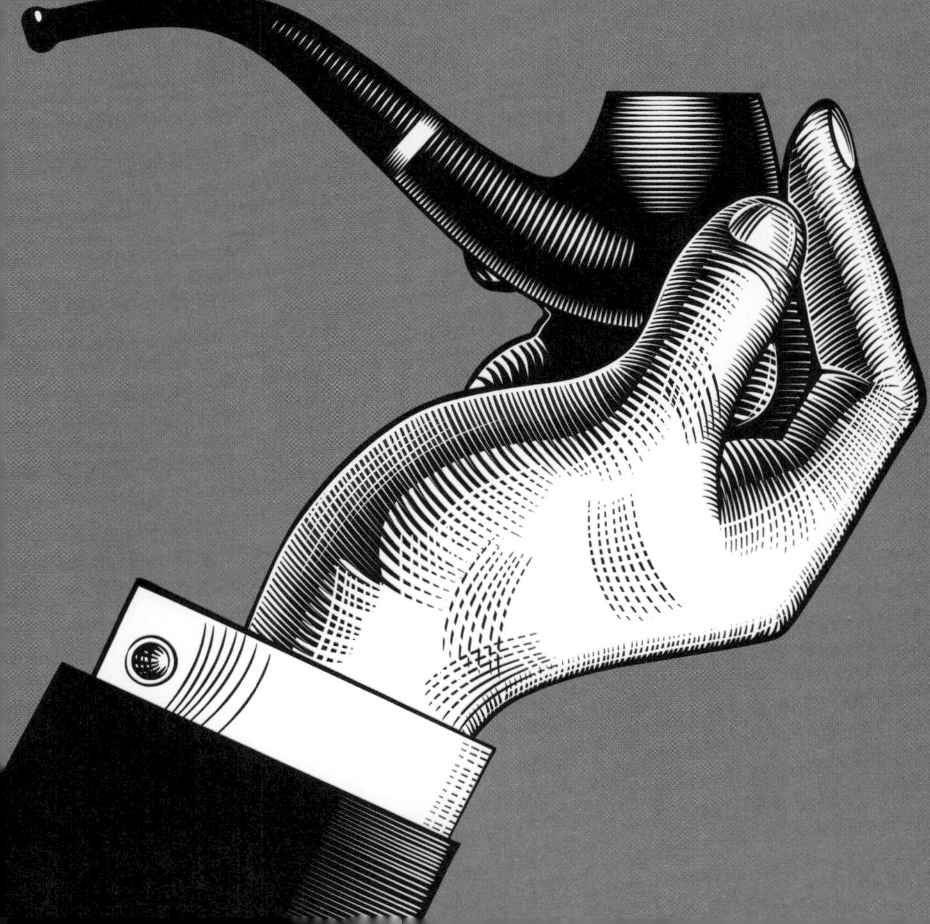

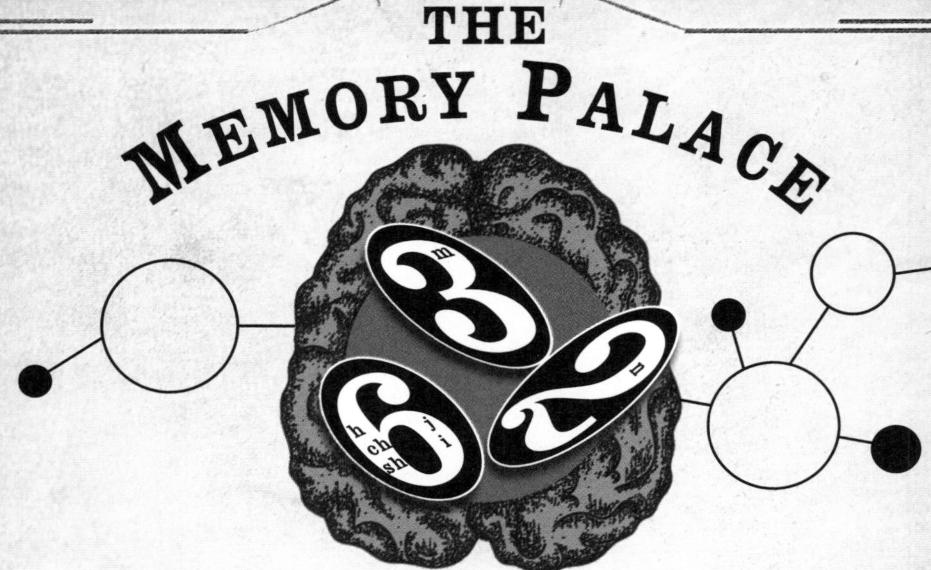

The Hérigone system

Holmes's next lecture was, I'll admit, a little intimidating, at least at first. His subsequent exercises took the matter more gently, as you'll see. Again, I have attempted to be as close to his words as possible.

It's time to progress deeper into the arts of memory, Watson. We've been mimicking natural mental processes so far, but now we're going to work on something more abstract, devised in the early 17th century by a French mathematician and astronomer named Pierre Hérigone. It is a method of memorising numbers, but it ties in closely with the techniques we have been working on so far.

The principle is quite simple. Each of the digits from 0 to 9 is associated with a small group of consonant sounds that are formed in the same broad place in the mouth and have a similar feel to their sound. A mnemonic image is created using a single-syllable word that contains just one of these consonant sounds, one that has at least some linking to the way the number is written. This image is then associated with its number in the usual manner.

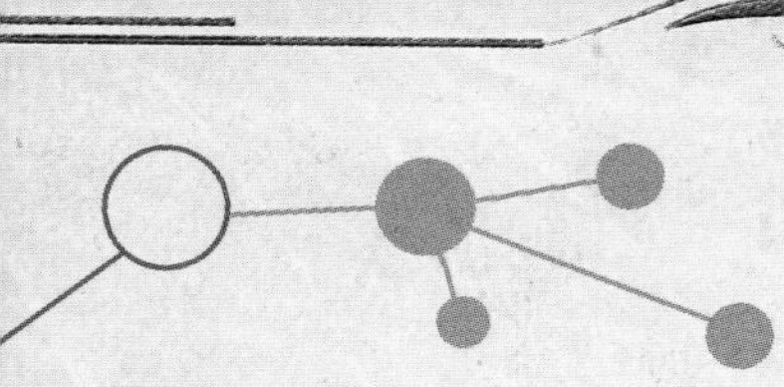

When the core 10 digits have been memorised, it is common to put in a little further effort to create images for the 90 numbers from 10 to 99, using imagery from words that have the appropriate two consonant sounds. Either way, once you have images for the numbers, you can chain them together vividly in sequences and then practise recall of the chain to remember a number of any given length.

Before anything else, you need to know the sounds associated with the numbers. Each of the sounds shown is a single noise; if the letters in a two-letter pair are pronounced separately, then they should be treated individually.

1 is the sounds *t*, *d*, *th*, and *dh*, as in **t**oe, **d**ie, **th**igh, and **th**y respectively.

2 is *n* and *ng*, as in **n**o and o**n**ion.

3 is *m* and *w*, as in **m**other and **w**eapon.

4 is *r*, rolled and unrolled, as in **r**oad or te**rr**or.

5 is just *l*, as in **l**ion.

6 is *j*, *ch*, *sh*, *sch*, *sc* and soft *g*, as in **j**ay, **ch**eer, **sh**ell, **sch**ool, **sc**ope and ra**ge**.

7 is *k*, *ck*, hard *c*, hard *g*, *q* and *x*, as in **kick**, **cog**, **q**uit and wa**x**.

8 is *f*, *ph*, *v* and soft *gh*, as in **f**ile, **ph**antasm, **v**ase and lau**gh**.

9 is *p* and *b*, as in **p**olish and **b**ath.

0, finally, is *s*, soft *c* and *z*, as in **s**igh, ri**c**e and di**zz**y.

You'll note that unvoiced letters and the vowels are all entirely absent from this schema. The various pronunciations of y are missing, as are the more continental uses of j, and – as fits a French system – the letter h. Do not be dismayed. The idea is to turn numbers into words, and not vice-versa.

It will take some study to memorise these attributions, but I will assist you.

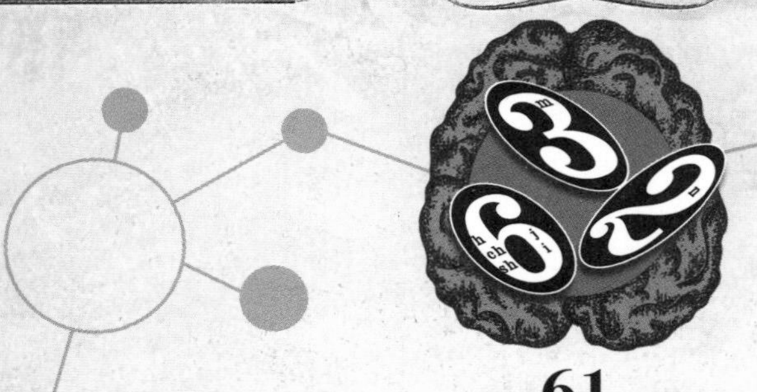

61

HÉRIGONE 1

I was reeling from Holmes's list of consonants and associated numbers. It was far too much to absorb.

Holmes patted me on the shoulder. "Don't take on so, old chap. Remember, the system is for memorising numbers, not words. Although a broader palette of options gives you a richer selection of choices, you only actually need one image for each number. That is eminently memorable, yes?"

"I suppose so," I agreed, and braced myself to jot some notes.

"Good man. So. Let's try the first five. The number 1 is long and straight, and associated with t. Capital T looks not unlike a tie, so 1 is a **tie**. If you turn 2 on its side, it is two vertical pieces connected with a diagonal stroke, like the N it associates with. A small n could be seen as the front legs, spine, and back legs of a horse, which is known for its **neigh**. For 3, a small m looks a little like a well-corseted maternal bosom seen from below, hence its association with mother, also known as **ma**. Next is 4, which ends with r, and looks slightly like a reversed capital R. To this I link a **ray** of light that shines in the shape of an X, with four arms. Finally we have 5, which is associated with L, the shape one makes if one holds up one's left hand, palm out, four fingers together with the lone thumb held away. A vulgar term, but I link this to a **loo**, specifically a lavatory designed so that the basin is a pentagon, with five sides."

I looked at my notepad. "1, T for tie. 2, N for neigh. 3, M for ma. 4, R for ray. 5, L for loo."

"Quite so. You should commit those to memory using the usual techniques. As an associated task, I would like you to ponder the following numbers, use their letter associations to turn them into consonant form, and then add such vowels and other omitted letters as required to convert them into English words or phrases. This will help you to start getting a feel for the utility of this technique."

He handed me a piece of paper, on which he'd written the numbers 142, 235, 4214, 52321 and 14325.

Only you know if you successfully blanked your loci route from last time, so, instead, can you find words to fit the numbers Holmes gave me?

SOLUTION ON PAGE 198

62

MIRROR MIRROR

I am not a particularly vain man. As a doctor, it is incumbent upon me to ensure that my appearance conveys a sense of reliability and security, and does not cause alarm, and it would be unprofessional of me to fail in this duty. Apart from that sole requirement, my appearance rarely crosses my mind. So when Holmes started interrogating me regarding mirrors, I was perhaps caught a little off guard.

"Watson! Does a mirror reverse your reflection horizontally, from left to right?"

I thought about that for a moment, and pictured looking into one of the things. "Yes," I ventured.

He shook his head. "Oh dear. Perhaps you'd like to think about the matter in greater depth."

I gave him a puzzled glance.

"Good man. While you're at it, tell me, what orientation of a flat mirror would also reverse your reflection vertically, in addition to its normal reversal?"

Perhaps you can tell me, in what manner does a mirror actually reverse your reflection normally, and how would you arrange one to also reverse you vertically?

SOLUTION ON PAGE 198

AMELIA

Mrs Hudson had brought up some afternoon tea and a plate of macaroons, but I thought I detected a glint of steely purpose in her eye as she wafted around the room, and I was not wrong.

"A curious thing, Doctor," she said to me.

"What's that?" I asked, bracing myself.

"My cousin Amelia lives in Bromley. That's not the curious part, though. If you add the ages of her three children together, they total the number on her door. If you multiply them, of course, you get 36. Interestingly, adding the ages together does not give a unique solution."

"Ah," I said.

"Now, obviously, that doesn't tell you everything, not quite, but her sister's lad, Alexander, is older than Amelia's trio."

"All right."

She smiled at me. "So an erudite man like yourself must be able to now tell me how old Alexander is without even visiting Bromley, given the lad's age is an even number."

Across the table, Holmes was watching me flounder with clear amusement.

How old is Alexander?

SOLUTION ON PAGE 198

64

WORKERS

"There's a little something in here that might serve you, Watson," Holmes said.

I looked over to see he was again engaged in reading one of his crime journals. "Ah," I said.

"There's a cautionary tale in here from Australia," he told me. "A pair of workmen were out gathering resources when they were attacked by vicious wildlife."

I nodded. "There's no shortage of that in Australia, from what I understand. Much of it startlingly venomous."

"Indeed so. On this occasion, venom was not involved. The two men retreated to safety. One, who kept his head and moved slowly, received a couple of nasty bites, but survived to make a full recovery. The other panicked and fled as fast as he could. The latter man was unharmed by the creatures and made it back to safety, but died shortly afterwards as a direct biological result of his actions. Can you deduce why?"

"Sounds ghastly," I said, and set to pondering.

Can you find the solution?

SOLUTION ON PAGE 199

65

PUB

We were eating breakfast one morning when Holmes said to me, "You know, I witnessed a rather odd event in Whitechapel last week."

The timing suggested he'd been digging into the Case of the Bewildering Banker, so my ears pricked up immediately. "Do tell."

"I was in the King's Head on Vallance Road, in the guise of a dissolute and decrepit drunkard, in order to observe a meeting of half a dozen men. After a mere five hours of my feigning unconsciousness in a corner, the group gathered, paying me no attention. A tense discussion ensued. After some minutes, a messenger lad came into the bar and instantly one of the men, clearly a bank clerk from Islington, leapt to his feet, darted across the room, and leapt through the front window."

"My word," I said. "How intemperate."

"Perhaps, Watson. Can you tell why the fellow took to his heels like that?"

What do you think?

SOLUTION ON PAGE 200

66

CHAMPAGNE

“Do you drink champagne, Watson?”

Random questions out of the blue were part and parcel of life at 221b, so I didn’t give it any thought. “On occasion, old chap. I prefer a glass of ale, to be honest, or a schooner of port.”

“I assume you’ve seen a bottle shaken before opening?”

I nodded. “Indeed, at the wedding of a friend of my father’s. It seemed a dreadful waste.”

“Why does shaking the bottle make a difference, do you think?”

I started to answer, then realised I was merely going to restate the question in a different way, and decided to ponder the matter instead.

Do you know the answer?

SOLUTION ON PAGE 200

67
HÉRIGONE 2

It had been a few days since Holmes had introduced me to the idea of associating numbers with letters, when he came over to me, tapped meaningfully on my notepad, and said, "You have your first five Hérigone pegs memorised now, I take it?"

I nodded. "Tie, neigh, ma, ray, loo."

"Excellent. Then it's time to consider six through to zero. The number 6 is linked to the letter j, and a capital J is not entirely unlike a mirrored, part-formed 6. I associate the number with an old **jaw** bone – one with just six teeth. Number 7 is k, and both can be imagined as lock-opening tools, the 7 as a bent wire used for a lockpick, and the k for a traditional **key**, with three teeth either side of the shaft, and one at the tip to make seven. Number 8 is f, which in cursive sometimes also comes with loops at top and bottom. The obvious word here is **foe**, of whom we have both seen plenty, armed with a pair of circular Hindu chakram throwing circles held vertically to form the digit. For 9, which is not unlike a small b rotated 180 degrees, I use a **bee**, one with nine stingers in a three by three square. Lastly, 0 corresponds to z, which 'zero' starts with, and so I associate that with a **zoo** – an empty one, naturally."

I had been duly noting the words, so was able to reel them off. "6, j for jaw. 7, k for key. 8, f for foe. 9, b for, well, bee. 0, z for zoo."

"Good work," Holmes said warmly. "Once again, you should practise recalling vivid mnemonic images for these associations until you have them locked in. In the meantime, I would like you to again practise associating numbers with letters by converting the following numbers into consonants, and then adding vowels and unrepresented letters as necessary to turn them into proper English. Do remember that this process works by sound, of course, and that other letters are open if needed."

I nodded. "Very well." He passed me a piece of paper which I accepted, and which bore the numbers 03487, 9412, 89471, 6947, 14271, 74071.

Can you find words to represent these numbers?

SOLUTION ON PAGE 201

68

BRINY

Investigating the Spitstone Bakery Affair, we came in contact with several Hookland mariners. Even by the very high standards of seafaring men worldwide, the sailors of that curious county are a veritable fountain of the most implausible tales.

One aged fellow with a face like hard-used leather told Holmes and I a strange, rambling tale of being blown north past Greenland. He described having to survive for a month on weevil-laden hard tack and melted sea-ice whilst he and his fellow crew engaged in a series of running battles against "seamen with long, claw-tipped arms".

It sounded like pure delirium of course, and I said as much to Holmes afterwards. Brine is not safe to drink, after all, and frozen saltwater is still saltwater.

Holmes gave me a quizzical look at that. "Oh?" he asked. "Are you quite sure?"

His tone of voice immediately suggested that I should think further.

Do you know what he was getting at?

SOLUTION ON PAGE 201

69

RULERSHIP

I was writing up notes on our latest foray into Hookland while Holmes puffed thoughtfully on his pipe. After a time, he turned his attention to me. "Do you happen to have a wooden ruler handy, Watson?"

I'd been including a few sketches in my notes, and, in fact, did have a ruler nearby. I picked the thing up and offered it to him.

Holmes shook his head. "It's not for me. I'd like you to try a little experiment."

"Oh?"

"Try balancing the ruler on your outstretched index fingers, so that it is horizontal."

"Very well," I said. It sounded convoluted, but in practice it was quite easy.

Holmes nodded. "That's it. Now try to slowly bring your index fingers together so that the ruler is sliding over both fingers at the same time."

I gave it a go, and failed. So I started over again, more carefully. I couldn't do it. "I'm missing a trick," I told Holmes. "I can't do it."

"It's not feasible," he told me.

"But do you know why not?"

SOLUTION ON PAGE 202

STARRY

I had just settled into a hard-earned hot bath one evening when Holmes's voice intruded on my weary reveries. His tone made it clear that he had decided this the most opportune moment to once again test my mental faculties. His reasoning, as he has explained to me at length in the past, is that crime will not pick an opportune moment to challenge me, and so neither should he.

Personally, I doubt that I will ever be called upon by circumstance to display mental ingenuity whilst sinking into a bath, but I suppose that is by the by.

"Watson! Why can you see stars?"

I admit that the best I could do as a retort was a befuddled, "What?"

"Light does not suddenly stop after travelling a certain distance. The universe is, we suppose, infinite. There are uncountable billions of stars."

"How can any point not be lit up? Why is the night sky not a blanket of white?"

SOLUTION ON PAGE 202

SPHERE

"You are sitting on a sphere, Watson," Holmes informed me one morning as I was cutting into a poached egg.

I blinked, and although I felt nothing, I leapt up to examine my chair. Not so much as a shelled pea was in evidence. "I am doing no such thing," I protested.

"The planet, my dear Watson. The planet. I admit it's not perfectly spherical, but it is very close."

I resumed my seat, and re-addressed myself to my egg with great forbearance, even if I say so myself.

Holmes was not put off in the slightest, of course. "If you spin a lump of clay on a potter's wheel at decent speed, it becomes a disk. So why is the Earth spherical?"

I lifted my chin at him in acknowledgement of the question, rather than spray him with egg, and gave the matter some thought.

What is your assessment?

SOLUTION ON PAGE 202

72

SAND ON THE BEACH

The coast immediately around Spitstone is surprisingly rocky, but there are pleasantly sandy coves just a couple of miles east of the town, and our investigations had landed us at a small tea shop at a beach overlooking one of the larger examples.

Holmes waited until I was in the process of biting into a scone – with jam and clotted cream, naturally – and then said, "You'll have noticed that when you walk on wet sand, it turns white around your foot. Why is that?"

I gulped my mouthful, and mumbled something about the water being squeezed out.

He actually tutted at me. "Sand is not a sponge, Watson. Try again."

What do you think?

SOLUTION ON PAGE 203

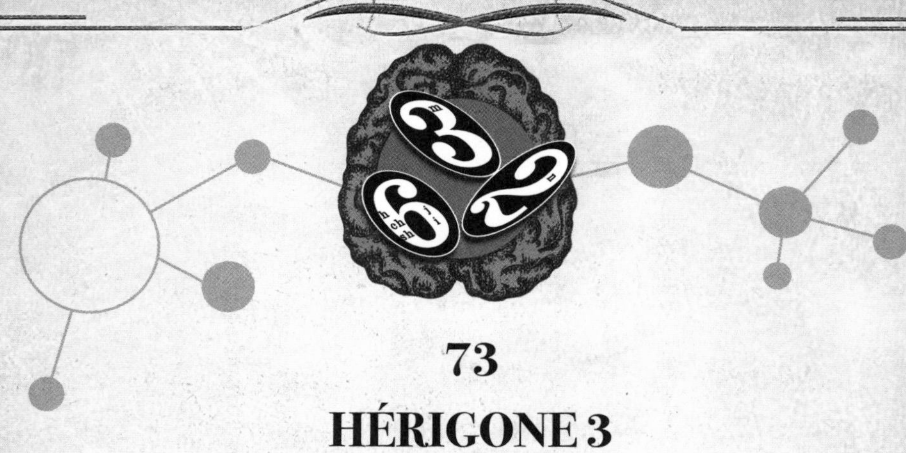

73
HÉRIGONE 3

I was almost happy with the speed of my recall of the Hérigone numbers when Holmes decided that I should push a little harder.

"Now that you've had a chance to memorise all the associations from 0 to 9, we should dip your toes into double digits."

"I don't entirely see the utility, old chap," I said. "If I'm turning a six-digit number into a word with a single image, what does it matter?"

"A valid question, Watson. I will demonstrate the utility shortly. Before I can do so however, you will need to memorise associations from 10 to 19."

I shrugged to myself. "Very well."

"In the interests of brevity, I will not belabour the principles behind the selected images. It should be plain. They start with 't', and feature the other appropriate consonant sound for the number. So, 10 is Lestrade in a **tizzy**, 11 is a **tot** in mother's arms, 12 is a **tin** of tobacco, 13 is a weighty **tome** about organic chemistry, 14 is a single **tear** trickling down a cheek, 15 is a **tool** – a magnifying glass to be precise, 16 is **Taj** for the Taj Mahal, 17 is an engorged **tick** on a dog's tail, 18 is a **toff** in a top hat and 19 is a **tub** for bathing in."

I repeated the associations I'd jotted down.

"Excellent. Get those memorised, and then we'll re-address the subject. Remember that you should also take the time to associate each single-digit number with the range of consonants it is associated with, not just the single ones we've concentrated on. As a demonstration of why that is useful, find associations for some other two-digit numbers."

He passed me over another note which held the numbers 75, 28, 44, 65, 80, 23, 39 and 96.

Can you find appropriate words for each?

SOLUTION ON PAGE 204

74

CRACK THE CODE

Holmes and I found ourselves, late one night, in a warehouse in Crouch End during the Affair of the Alderman's Trout. A small group of villains were using the place as a secure storage, but as their failure to notice either of us attests, they were not particularly good at security. Obviously one of them was new, because the others were making him learn a numerical combination lock code by attempting to guess it.

At Holmes's suggestion, I recorded his trials and what he was told each time, so that I can present them here. The below are just a selection of his attempts, but they contain sufficient information for you to find the solution.

206 : 2 numbers from the code but in the wrong places

645 : 1 number from the code but in the wrong place

682 : 1 correct number in the right place

738 : completely wrong

780 : 1 number from the code but in the wrong place

What is the correct code?

SOLUTION ON PAGE 204

OWLS

"I want you to imagine an antiques salesman." Holmes watched me expectantly.

I settled back in my armchair and did as I was instructed. My salesman was a slightly oleaginous fellow, with slicked-back hair and a slyly ingratiating smile. I did not like him overmuch, and wondered why my mind had chosen to create him. Then it occurred to me that it was, after all, my mind, so I erased him and produced a different image, a far more pleasant-looking chap.

"All settled to your satisfaction?" Holmes asked.

"Quite, thank you," I said.

"Capital. Let us suppose that this salesman purchases a small carving of an owl for six shillings in the morning, and sells it to another dealer for seven shillings at lunchtime. Shortly afterwards, he is offered nine shillings for such a piece by an owl enthusiast, so he buys it back from the other dealer for eight shillings and closes the deal with the enthusiast. What is his profit on the piece?"

I had to think through the tangles before I had an answer I was happy with.

What do you make it?

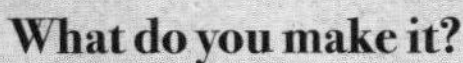

SOLUTION ON PAGE 204

76

TIDE

I was cleaning my service revolver one evening when Holmes appeared next to me out of nowhere and thrust a large, ripe orange in front of my nose. "Tides!" he declared.

I am not too proud to admit that I recoiled sharply from the unexpected fruit.

Holmes peered at me, as if somewhat concerned. "It's only an orange, my dear Watson. Nothing to be alarmed by."

"My apologies," I managed.

"Think nothing of it," he said magnanimously. "You know, I trust, that there are two high tides each day at any given tidal location, and that when it is high tide at one point, it is also high tide at the equivalent spot on the opposite side of the Earth, assuming of course that both locations are tidal."

I nodded. "Indeed."

"Why?" He set the orange down next to my revolver's barrel.

Do you know the answer?

SOLUTION ON PAGE 205

FLY

Holmes and I had recently returned from a foray in to Kensington in the matter of the Culpepper Murder. I was sitting by the window with a very pleasant cup of tea, idly watching a fly walk up the pane.

Holmes, seated opposite, noticed my object of attention.

"Curious, isn't it," he said. "They can even stand on the ceiling. Geckos can as well. You may have seen it."

"In Afghanistan, yes. Not many geckos roaming London, alas."

"Do you know how flies do it? It's not because their feet are coated in anything sticky."

"I haven't given it much thought," I said.

Holmes nodded. "Now would be an opportune moment to do so."

How do they do it?

SOLUTION ON PAGE 205

APPLES

"Undue carelessness has undone many a man, Watson. Complacency is often the enemy of life and health, even in the most innocuous of circumstances."

"Oh?" I looked around the room, seeking for some clue as to the source of this outburst.

Holmes waved one of his criminal journals at me. "There's a story in this volume recounting the fate of a neglectful gardener. This poor fellow had a couple of fruit trees, and went out one afternoon to pick some of the produce. He was careless, and fell. Completely pulverised most of his skeleton."

"That's terrible," I said. "Some sort of brittle bone disease?"

"Not in the least. Perfectly healthy when it happened."

"That's an amazing amount of damage falling from a tree. How tall are they?"

"Less than 10 feet," he said.

I shook my head. "It's not possible."

"I assure you it's not only possible, it's perfectly simple."

He was right, too.

How did it happen?

SOLUTION ON PAGE 205

79

HÉRIGONE 4

"You've memorised the Hérigone pegs up to 19, I take it?"

It was a few days afterwards, and I had indeed. I nodded.

"Good. I want to show you why I have been pushing you regarding two-digit associations. Have a go at finding a word for, say, 96678."

Let me spare you: I couldn't find a word for bjjkf. I eventually had to admit defeat.

Holmes nodded. "It's much quicker, in almost all cases of wanting to remember numbers, to chain together a series of mnemonics you already know than to take the time to devise and memorise a suitably visual word or set of words for a number of even moderate length."

"I can see that," I said.

"So the trick is to break a longer number into numbers you already have memorised, and then chain it together along a route of loci. If you have firm associations for every number up to 99, your chain will be approximately half the length of a chain built on just 0 to 9, and thus require half the effort. It's also less repetitious than always using the same 10 mnemonics. In addition, you automatically have mnemonic imagery you can use to clearly number the items in a list you want to remember, or to number the stops along your route, or to enumerate quantities. This is a very versatile tool, and I strongly recommend putting in the effort to devise and remember two-digit pegs to 99, and don't forget 00 to 09 either. Going up to 999 and beyond is only for those with a natural aptitude, but up to 99 is for everyone."

"As a proof of the point, I'd like you to create linked mnemonic chains for three eight digit numbers, and time each endeavour. For the first, use the double-digit associations from 10 to 19. For the second, use the single-digit associations from 0 to 9. And for the third, devise as few words as possible and chain those."

The numbers he handed me were 18141913, 25387609 and 49583160.

How long do they take you?

SOLUTION ON PAGE 206

80

JUGGED

I still recall the moment clearly. It was a Sunday, an hour after a most pleasant luncheon, and I was just nodding off. A pair of loud thumps beside me and some worrying sloshes jolted me straight to full consciousness. I looked over to see Holmes had placed a pair of large, heavy jugs haphazardly on the table beside my armchair. I was blinking at them in confusion when he handed me a half-pint mug liberated, I assume, from a public house.

"This jug—" he tapped the leftmost "—holds a pint of water. The other, a pint of milk."

My alarm at this point was starting to recede, and I nodded.

"I would like you to use your glass to pour a half-pint of milk into the water and, after mixing it around, to then pour a half-pint of the mixture back into the milk so the two jugs are level again."

I did so, with almost no audible muttering.

"Now, please repeat the procedure."

Once again, I obeyed.

"I trust that it is clear that the amount of water in one jug is equal to the amount of milk in the other. However, I would like you to tell me how many more times you will need to repeat the half-pint back and forth in order to have exactly half milk and half water in both jugs?"

Do you know the answer?

SOLUTION ON PAGE 206

WAVY

It was a blustery afternoon, and Holmes and I were on Marylebone Road, heading back to Baker Street from Euston. A policeman on a horse went clopping past us, and turned off towards the park. As the horse's steps slowly faded, Holmes turned to me with a look of calculation.

"You know the term 'sound wave' I assume, Watson."

"Yes," I said. "The idea that sound moves through the air in a manner similar to the way a wave moves across the surface of the sea."

"And are you aware that light also behaves like a wave?"

"I am, although I seem to recall some doubts arising as to the nature of the aether it travels through."

"Indeed," he said dryly. "As you can still hear, the sound from the horse is perfectly capable of diffracting – turning the corner – to reach us. So why do you imagine it is that we cannot also see round corners?"

What do you think?

SOLUTION ON PAGE 207

PENNIES

Holmes had set Wiggins and the Baker Street Irregulars to watching associates of the Alderman whose trout were proving so troublesome. The lad found us one afternoon in Regent's Park, and after sharing his intelligence with Holmes, he turned to me with a cheeky grin.

"Fancy a little challenge, Doctor?" he asked.

I smiled at the boy. "Why not?"

"Champion. I've got 26 coins in my pouch. If I took out 20 of them, I'd have at least one halfpenny, at least two pennies, and at least five two-penny bits. So how about you either tell me how much I've got in there in total, or give me a shilling?"

My smile became fixed, I'm sure, but I gamely told Wiggins I'd give him the shilling either way, and set about trying to calculate the answer.

Can you figure it out?

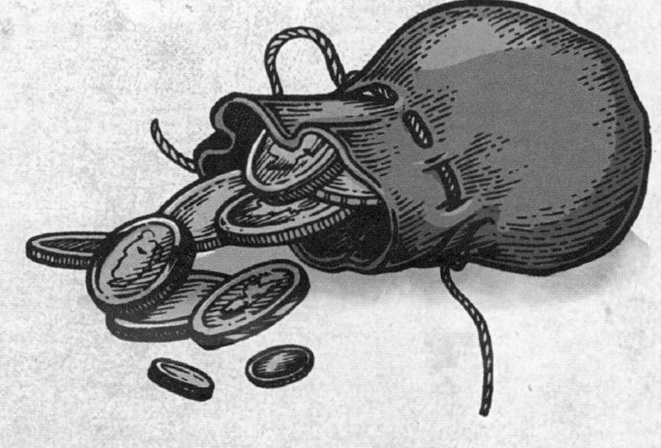

SOLUTION ON PAGE 207

83

STAINLESS

"Stainless steel really is a wonderful thing," Mrs Hudson said to me one afternoon, having just provided us with a fresh pot of tea. "It's lovely not to have to scour the rust off every week."

Holmes nodded absently, so I thought I'd try to be encouraging. "It does sound like a significant improvement, Mrs Hudson."

She beamed at me. "Oh, it is. And being a man of science as you are, I'm sure you know exactly how it is that it stays rust-free."

"Well, I..." I began.

"Please, do tell me," she said, a faint grin creeping around the corners of her expectant expression.

She stood there patiently while Holmes chuckled quietly and I racked my memory.

Do you know the answer?

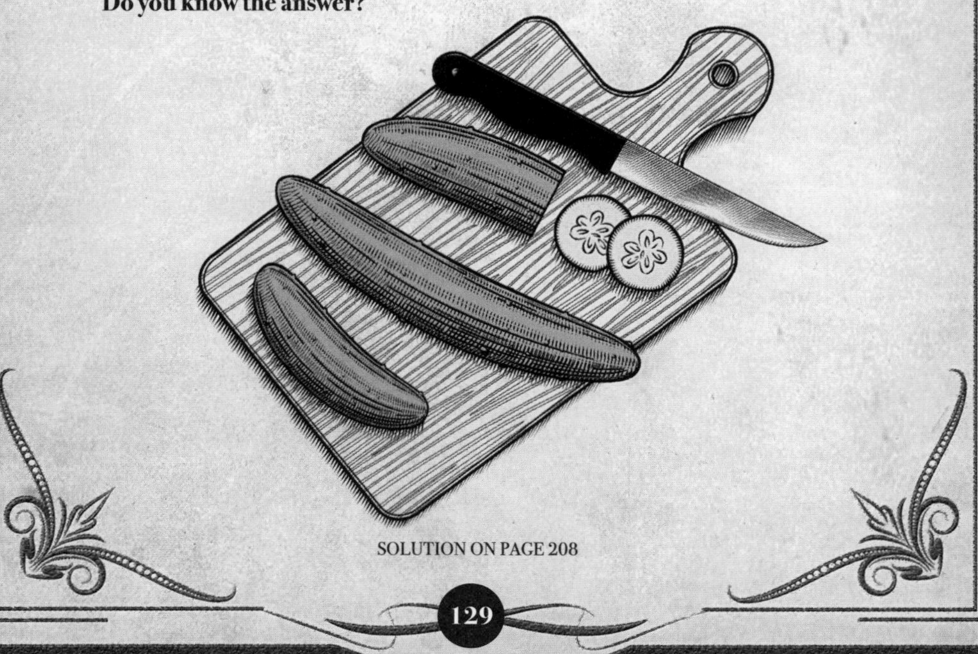

SOLUTION ON PAGE 208

SMITHS

Mrs Hudson passed me a slice of her Church Window Cake, a very fancy multi-coloured chequerboard affair held together with apricot jam and marzipan. "This will brighten your afternoon, Doctor."

"Thank you kindly, my dear lady," I said. "It looks exquisite."

"By the by, that reminds me," she said. "Did I ever mention my cousin Hetty?"

"Honestly, I'm not entirely sure," I admitted.

"She married a fellow called Ted Smith, a Surrey lad with hair the colour of gold and eyes like sapphires. Daft as a stack of brushes, mind you. Still. They have six now, and plenty of them girls."

I wondered where this was going, if anywhere. "I see," I lied.

"Well, Doctor. Let me tell you, if you meet any two of Hetty's girls, there's exactly an even chance that they'll both have Ted's blue eyes. That means you should be able to tell me how many daughters the Smiths have, and how many of them have blue eyes."

Can you find the solution?

SOLUTION ON PAGE 208

Initialling

To my relief, Holmes's next memory technique, initialling, was significantly less intricate than the previous one.

After the rigours of the Hérigone system, my dear Watson, I've readied something a little simpler for you. To restate an earlier point, the memory works best by repetition of recall, rather than by repetition of observation.

For best results, these repetitions should be spaced out over increasing amounts of time. You don't want the information clogging up your thought processes, you just want it at your fingertips when you need it. That means getting your brain used to shunting it from long-term storage back to your awareness, and then tidying it away again. So you recall every few minutes, then every few hours, every day, every few days, and so on.

I am revisiting this because it is particularly important for the technique of initialling. Memorising verbatim text is a stern challenge for the memory. When we read, we remember the sense of the material far more readily than the precise words used – we turn the text into a sort of

story, which is always how our minds best remember. But sometimes that is not sufficient, and we have to learn the exact phraseology.

The challenge with a passage of text is giving the mind enough material in the short-term memory that you can start practising its recall. There are options available to you here. For many, the most effective method is to copy the passage out by hand, possibly more than once. Others swear by reading the text aloud, sometimes to a musical or poetic rhythm, or by having a third party read the text to you. Sometimes, good results can be obtained by treating the material as an exercise in summary.

Whatever option you choose, the point here is not to learn the piece outright, but merely to familiarise your mind with it. Once you have a sense of the text, you are to write it out again on a clean sheet of paper, this time recording only the first letter of each word. These initials serve as prompts to your mind so that you can recall the precise words.

Once you have your sheet of initialled text, practise reading through it as you would recalling any other mnemonic. When you go wrong, take a piece of scrap paper and write out five words from the passage with the incorrect word as the centre word and re-initial the five beneath that. Then restart that recall.

In a few days, you will find you can recall the text perfectly from the initials. At that point, move to reciting it – or writing it, if you prefer – entirely from memory. Soon you will have it held fast.

Texts of any length can be committed to memory this way, but I would suggest memorising them in chunks no longer than 500 to 1000 words.

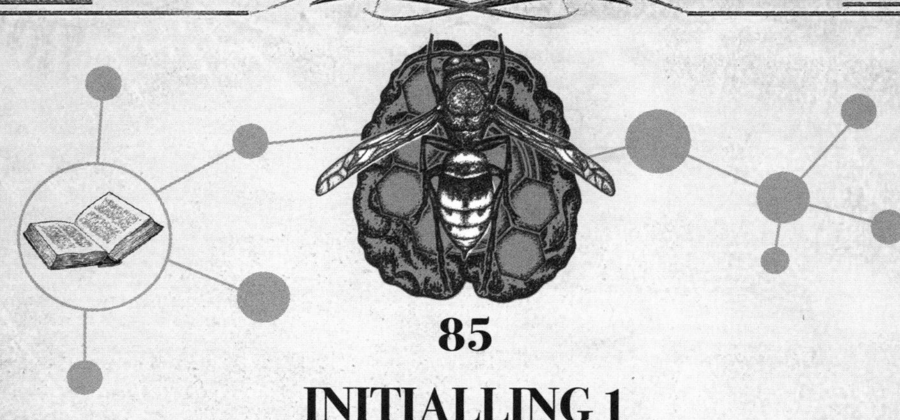

85

INITIALLING 1

"Well then, Watson, you have the principle of memorising text?"

I confirmed that I did indeed.

"Then let us put it into practice. For your first effort, I have selected a modest piece of Shakespeare – the start of Antony's speech from Act 3 of *Julius Caesar*. I suggest reading it out loud, then copying it out fully, and finally turning it into a set of initials. Preserve the punctuation and line structure, as that will help it bed into your memory."

He handed me a sheet of paper, with the selection he'd mentioned on it.

Friends, Romans, countrymen, lend me your ears;
I come to bury Caesar, not to praise him.
The evil that men do lives after them;
The good is oft interred with their bones;
So let it be with Caesar. The noble Brutus
Hath told you Caesar was ambitious:
If it were so, it was a grievous fault,
And grievously hath Caesar answered it.
Here, under leave of Brutus and the rest –
For Brutus is an honourable man;
So are they all, all honourable men –
Come I to speak in Caesar's funeral.
He was my friend, faithful and just to me:
But Brutus says he was ambitious;
And Brutus is an honourable man.

Once you have also read aloud and then copied the text, how does your initialling come out?

SOLUTION ON PAGE 209

RACE

The matter of the Culpepper Murder was significantly confused by the will, and initially by the pressing absence thereof. Holmes, in particular, took the problem as a personal affront, one that served only to distract him from more significant issues. Once we had retrieved the will – from the bottom of a specific pew in the Temple Church, of all places – its contents added an extra dollop of bedevilment to the lives of the victim's sons.

Culpepper had owned a selection of fine thoroughbred racehorses, and gave the best two, an evenly-matched pair of three-year-olds, to his sons, one horse each. His will then decreed that the sons would race their horses over a course on Culpepper's estate to decide which of them received the great majority of his remaining wealth and possessions. The rub was that while the race was required to be fair, it was the owner of the losing horse who would inherit.

Both sons immediately kicked up a stink, of course, pre-emptively accusing the other of throwing the race by all sorts of devious means. Lestrade was quite beside himself, which only added to Holmes's annoyance.

"The matter is so simple that even Watson could resolve it," he eventually snapped at the poor inspector.

This was news to me, but after a while, I did manage to come up with a strategy by which a competitive race could be ensured.

What is it?

SOLUTION ON PAGE 209

87

ROSEMARY

Mrs Hudson placed a rack of toast on the table between Holmes and me, and fixed us with a carefully mild expression that I had come to recognise as one of her little tests. As I have mentioned elsewhere, I used to believe that she took pride in the speed of Sherlock's mental prowess, but I have come to the suspicion that she was in cahoots with him in the matter of my forcible mental betterment.

Sure enough, she started in on a head-scratcher of a tale.

"My young niece, Rosemary, has the boys on her street eating out of her hand. Just last week, I overhead her engaging a pair of them in some complicated game. Two regular whole numbers she'd written down, consecutive ones bigger than nought, and she'd told one of them to a lad named Alf, and the other to a boy called Simon. They're both sharp, no doubt about that. So while herself prances around, Alf says to Simon, 'I don't know what your number is.' Simon nods, thinks for a moment, and says, 'Then I don't know what your number is.' So Alf thinks a bit longer, and then he grins, and says, 'That means I know your number now.' And Simon grins back, and says, 'Well, then I know your number too.' Quite the thing it was. And then the three of them dash off for the next part in their odd game. Now, Doctor, I don't have the first idea what either of Rosemary's numbers were, but I'm sure you can tell me one of them, as learned as you are."

I sighed and tried to start making sense of it all.

Can you deduce the solution?

SOLUTION ON PAGE 210

BROTHERS

I was catching up on the day's news one evening, having been too busy to read the newspaper during the day. Some nasty business was taking place in India again; as usual, the poor devils who belonged there were getting the worst of it.

"I want to engage your imagination with an implausibility, my dear Watson," Holmes said from across the room.

I looked up from the paper with a certain relief. "It would be my pleasure."

"How encouraging. Pray, conjure up a pair of twin brothers, and encumber them with significant mental and cognitive problems, to wit, have one of them an obligate liar, and the other an obligate truth-teller. Furthermore, let us assume that the truth-teller is correct in all his suppositions, whilst his lying brother is inaccurate in all of his. That is, if a statement is true, the truth-teller believes it to be true, and the liar believes it to be false."

"How ghastly," I said.

Holmes shrugged. "Probably. I trust you can see that both brothers will provide the same answer to the same yes/no question. If you ask them, one lunchtime, if it is currently night, the honest one will know that it is not and say 'no', but the liar will think that it is, and lie to you, also saying 'no'. But let us suppose you meet one of the pair, and want to ascertain which is which. Can you devise a yes or no question that would give you the answer?"

I had to give that some considerable thought.

Can you think of a suitable question?

SOLUTION ON PAGE 210

WRONG TROUSERS

"I say, Watson. Have you ever considered reversing your trousers whilst bound?"

I spluttered, and looked over at Holmes, who was the very picture of innocent inquiry. "What the devil do you mean by that?" I demanded.

"Not a word more than I've said."

"I... Well... That is, no. No, I have not."

"It's time to start."

I felt myself going a little pale. "Whatever do you mean, old chap?"

"Imagine, if you will, that there is a few feet of rope tied between your ankles and that, for any reason you care to contrive, you need to turn your trousers inside out and put them back on, with the button still at the front."

"This is one of your mental exercises?" I'm sure the relief was plain on my voice.

"Yes, Watson, do try to keep up. How would you go about the process without cutting the rope or damaging your trousers?"

"I... Very well, Holmes."

Do you know how it can be done?

SOLUTION ON PAGE 211

ST MARY'S AXE

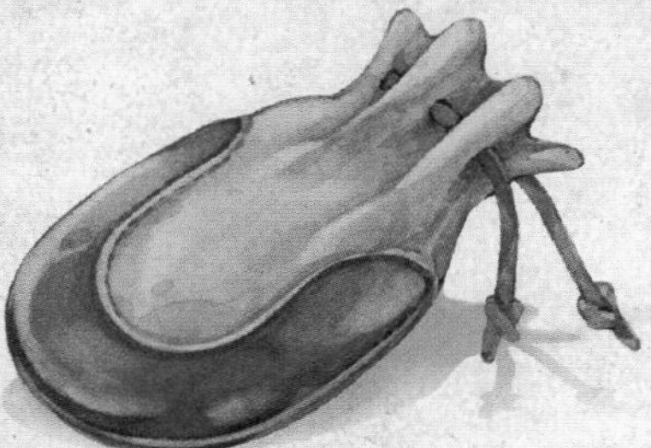

During the Case of the Bewildering Banker, Holmes and I found ourselves loitering outside a building on St Mary's Axe. We were dressed for the location, complete with sombre morning suits, Chesterfield coats and silk top hats. We made a quite plausible pair of bankers, I dare say. Either way, no-one gave us a second glance for the couple of hours we were there.

About halfway through, Holmes surprised me by pulling out a leather pouch and waggling it at me in a curious manner.

I stared at him.

He was utterly unabashed. "Let us suppose this pouch contains a number of identical black balls and one single white ball that is otherwise identical to its brethren."

"If you like," I said.

"Let us say that we were to play a game where we each took turns to randomly draw a ball from the bag and keep it, with the first person to draw the white ball being the victor. Would it be advantageous to go first or second?"

"Um," I said, cleverly.

What do you think?

SOLUTION ON PAGE 211

SECTION FOUR

HARD

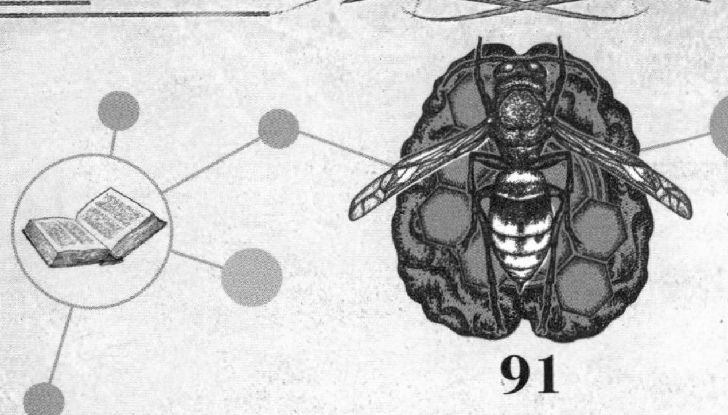

91

INITIALLING 2

A few days after I'd abbreviated Mark Antony's speech from *Julius Caesar*, Holmes came over to me bearing the piece of paper I had used in the process, and handed it to me.

"Here, Watson," he said. "Do you remember the words?"

F, R, c, l m y e;
l c t b C, n t p h.
T e t m d l a t;
T g i o i w t b;
S l i b w C. T n B
H t y C w a;
l i w s, i w a g f,
A g h C a i.

It turned out that I did, somewhat to my surprise.

Holmes beamed at me. "Excellent, old chap. But obviously, if you need a speech memorised verbatim, it is expected you will not have a sheet of reminder letters. So the next stage is to cut the number of reminders. So I would like you to revise your note. Cross out the second and third letter of every trio, and re-copy, without punctuation. For Shakespeare, whose lines are short, re-start your count with each new line, so you always have the first letter of the line. As always, practice using it to recall the full speech several times, at staggered periods."

I set about my task.

How does it come out when you do it – and can you recall the full text?

SOLUTION ON PAGE 212

92

BALLOONS

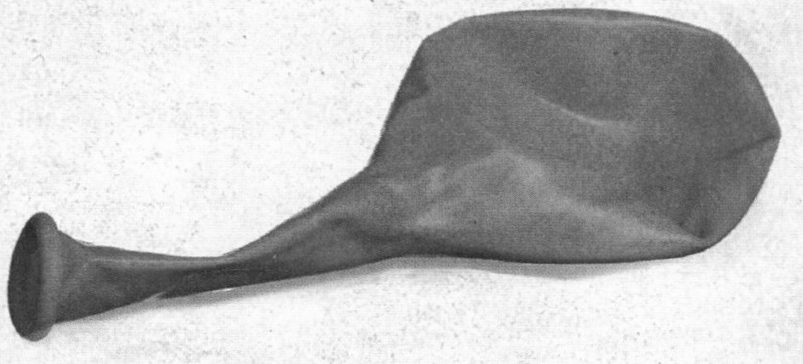

"The mind knows far more than any man can be aware of," Holmes told me. "It is prone to performing calculations behind the scenes, where you're not aware of them, and just handing you the answer out of nowhere. The difference between a reliable burst of intuition and an idle fancy can be subtle, however. It takes practice to differentiate them, but if you keep working to hone the faculty, your intuition can become a scalpel of certainty. So it is important to challenge your intuitive abilities."

I nodded. It was not the first time Holmes had expressed such sentiments to me.

"Imagine I were to pass you two party balloons, Watson, one completely deflated and one already half-filled with air. Which do you feel would be the easier to blow into a dozen times?"

My intuition must have been asleep on the job, for I had no ready answer.

What do you think?

SOLUTION ON PAGE 212

FOUL

"Here's an interesting witness statement for you to consider, my dear Watson." Holmes was brandishing one of his salacious periodicals at me.

I put down the volume of Pepys I was reading and endeavoured to look attentive. "Oh?"

He tossed me the magazine, and directed me to the second column of the right-hand page. It discussed the testimony of one Anthony Borrell in the investigation into the murder of George Frederick Alberson of Kingston. Nothing within it leapt out as warranting my particular attention:

"At 9.50pm, I was walking up Rook's Lane. It's a dingy alley, but it's perfectly safe, running alongside the graveyard. I always take it home. The victim was some fifteen yards in front of me, headed the same way, and I hadn't paid him two thoughts. Then, as he passed the old Lich Gate, a burly, bearded man with red hair stepped out of the darkness to stand in front of the victim. The red-haired man put a friendly hand on the other's shoulder, and then swiftly drove a slender ice-pick up under the unfortunate man's chin. As the victim collapsed, the killer retrieved his weapon and vanished back into the shadows. I'm not ashamed to admit that I turned tail and ran all the way back to the other end of Church Street, and didn't stop until I saw a bobby."

"Thoroughly unpleasant," I said to Holmes.

He arched an eyebrow at me. "Really, Watson? Were you paying attention?"

What had I missed?

SOLUTION ON PAGE 213

HOW MANY COWS

Whilst we were investigating the Spitstone Bakery Affair, the good people of the county of Hookland seemed much taken with a set of mysterious cow deaths that had occurred during the recent storms. Holmes, who was attempting to gather information surreptitiously, encouraged this gossip relentlessly.

It seemed to me that the lightning strikes observed during these storms were an obvious culprit, but some of the details did admittedly appear somewhat odd.

For example, one farmer insisted that he was standing beneath a tree when it was lightning-struck, and felt a certain discomfort, but when he emerged, he found that ones of his cows had died. It was clearly further from the impact point than he had been. Another man attested that he'd rushed to where lightning had struck near his herd, and found that some animals near the strike were utterly unharmed, while others next to them had dropped dead. Many of the locals put this caprice down to malicious sprites.

On the second evening, in the taproom of The Electric Messiah, Holmes broke character quietly to ask for my explanation of the events.

What do you think?

SOLUTION ON PAGE 213

95

AMAZING

I was sitting at the dining table one lazy Saturday afternoon, reading the papers, when Holmes appeared from his study, clutching a blank piece of paper.

"Whatever do you have there?" I asked.

"An imaginary maze, my dear Watson."

"Beastly," I said, a hint of suspicion kindling inside me.

"My maze operates under certain rules. It is a twenty-three by twenty-three grid of square rooms, each of which contains an arrow indicating up, right, down, or left. You may exit only in the direction of the arrow. As you move into the new room, the old room rotates ninety degrees clockwise. If the direction of the arrow would lead beyond the walls of the maze, the arrow continues turning until it points to another cell. There is precisely one room that permits escape, through the floor."

"If I may, old chap, I'll revise my opinion downwards from beastly to positively fiendish."

Holmes continued inexorably. "Let us suppose that a thousand Watsons are placed into a thousand such mazes, each one with its initial arrows set entirely at random."

"My word!"

"How many Watsons will eventually escape?"

Do you know?

SOLUTION ON PAGE 213

MALFEASANCE

Wiggins had an uncommonly grave expression on his face when we met him one afternoon in St James's Park. After providing Holmes with an enigmatic piece of information concerning an unpleasant-sounding place by the name of "Rat Island", he accepted his due payment with a sigh that, on reflection, may have been a tad theatrical.

It was most strange to see the scamp with anything other than a cheeky grin fixed in place. "Is everything quite all right?" I asked him.

"It's the deception I object to, Doctor," he replied. "One of the Irregulars based in Soho pinched something unwise from a theatre. That's fine, it happens. But when I investigated the matter, more than half a dozen of them lied to me. John told me it was James. Gertie told me she did it. Bessie told me Gertie was lying. Simon told me both Gertie and John were lying. Mark told me it was Bessie. Donald told me it was neither him nor Bessie. Kitty told me that Mark, Donald and herself were all innocent. James told me it was either Bessie or Simon. Fred told me John and James were lying. Leonard told me that out of Simon, Mark and Donald, only one was telling the truth. And Flora told me that out of the

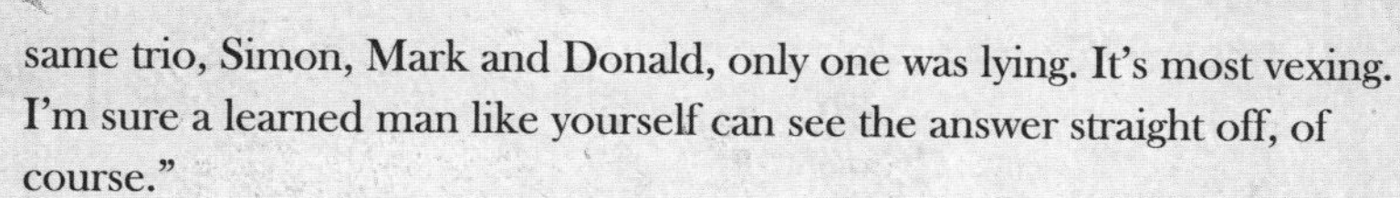

same trio, Simon, Mark and Donald, only one was lying. It's most vexing. I'm sure a learned man like yourself can see the answer straight off, of course."

He looked at me expectantly.

Can you figure out the culprit?

SOLUTION ON PAGE 213

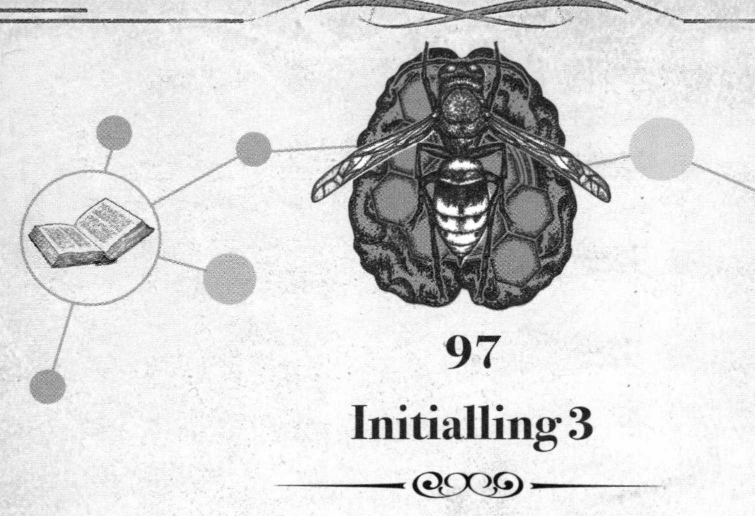

97

Initialling 3

Holmes presented me with my doubly-abbreviated notes for Mark Antony's speech a few days after I had prepared it. "Still remember this, old friend?"

Fle
Ibt
Tma
Tot
SbT
HC
Isa
AC

It was early in the morning, and I was not really prepared to have notebook thrust at me, but I rallied well, even if I say so myself. I fumbled a little over one word, but otherwise, I recalled the fragment.

"Excellent work," Holmes said. "The last step in this process is to meld each of these small groups of letters into a mnemonic image, and then practice recalling the images as you would any other list, with the aid of your path of loci. I suggest starting off your list with a reminder of the play itself, to firm up the context. Altering the initial image of the loci is a good way to hang a specific list onto the path. Remember to also occasionally practice recalling the letters associated with the image, and the words associated with the letters. You should find these come readily however, having already shown your memory that you are interested in them several times."

I settled down to do as I was bid, and prepare a list of mnemonic images.

Can you do the same – and can you recall the fragment of speech indicated above?

SOLUTION ON PAGE 214

THIEVES

I was addressing myself to a slice of well-deserved toast when I realised that Holmes had turned a fixed gaze upon me. I swallowed my mouthful. "Yes, old chap?"

He offered me a slightly predatory smile. "My dear Watson, there is a stern matter of theoretical robbers. Three of them."

"Well then," I said. "We'd best be afoot. Theoretically."

"You should be aware also of the three sisters they stole from, and the three jewels that were stolen."

"A trio of trios," I noted. "Very well."

"So then. I will tell you this. The man who stole the diamond was a bachelor, and the most dangerous of the thieves. Anna was younger than the sister who owned the emerald. Richard, who stole from the eldest sister and was less dangerous than the man who took the emerald, was Thomas's brother-in-law. The man who stole from Anna had no brothers or sisters. Thomas did not steal from Francine. Finally, you also need to know that there was a ruby, a thief named Harold, and a sister named Sophie. Armed with this information, you will be fully able to tell me which man took which gem from which sister."

"Will I, by God?"

Holmes nodded gravely.

Do you know who took what from which sister and how dangerous he was?

SOLUTION ON PAGE 215

99

LENS

Holmes had been minutely examining a small silver grasshopper with inset chips of ruby for several minutes, so that he might more precisely place the location of its fashioning. Eventually he straightened. "Jaffa," he declared. "The legs are quite distinctive." Then he seemed to notice the magnifying glass in his hand. "I need not question your familiarity with the humble hand lens, old friend. So tell me, instead, of telescopes."

I stared at Holmes for a moment, then shrugged mentally. "Of telescopes? Very well. Long chaps, chiefly metallic, lenses at—"

"Permit me to halt your explanations there, Watson. I meant, instead, of their actual functioning. Would you say that they make distant sights appear larger or nearer? Those two effects are not identical."

That had me at a loss for a while.

What do you think?

SOLUTION ON PAGE 216

100

ROBBERS

"Rhetorical thieves are a serious business," Holmes told me sternly.

"I believe you implicitly," I assured him.

"Consider the matter of the golden Pegasus. When it was retrieved, by a fellow named Alexander, it was clear that either Bernard or Charles was the thief. The matter was complicated by the nature of the assorted testimonies gathered from assorted witnesses and cognoscenti, whose names, you will observe, are alphabetically convenient."

"Useful things, rhetorical witnesses," I observed.

"Quite so. The following claims were recorded. Derek said that Bernard did not steal the Pegasus. Edward observed that Bernard had stolen items in the past. Francis pointed out that Charles had also stolen. Graham weighed in to unpleasantly note that Francis too was a known thief. Henry claimed that both Edward and Francis were correct. Ian said that at least one of Francis and Graham was correct. James maintained that it was Edward or Graham who were both correct. Liam believed that at least one of Henry and James was correct. Kendry said that Edward and Ian were both correct. Alexander, finally, put in his belief, that Liam was correct and Kendry was wrong."

"Hm."

"Never fear, Watson. If I tell you that Alexander and Derek are either both correct or both incorrect, the matter becomes quite simple."

"Hm," I repeated.

Can you figure out the guilty party?

SOLUTION ON PAGE 216

METEORIC

One rainy morning, I was walking towards Harley Street with Holmes, who was going on towards Bloomsbury to speak with a singular artist. I was cold, tired, and wet of face, so naturally Holmes seized on my indisposition as the perfect time to engage my critical faculties.

"You've seen shooting stars, my dear Watson," he said.

"Many times," I replied. "I saw some very impressive showers of them in the small hours of the morning, when I was on night duty in Afghanistan."

"Surely you don't imagine that such timing is coincidence."

I shrugged. "I haven't given the matter much thought."

"Do so," he suggested. "And let me know what you deduce."

What do you think?

SOLUTION ON PAGE 217

WIRE

"May I claim your attention for a moment?" Holmes asked me.

It was late afternoon, and I was not doing anything particularly pressing, so I nodded, and turned to face him.

He brandished a perfectly normal sheet of blank paper at me, the sort one might use to write a letter. "This is an entirely regular piece of paper," he said.

I nodded.

He gravely put both his hands – and of course the paper – behind his back, watching me intently, for something like half a minute. Then he produced the paper again with a flourish, and to my astonishment it bore a distinct chicken-wire pattern, having been creased into a perfectly-fitting sheet of hexagons. He passed the paper to me to examine more closely. "How did I do that, Watson? I assure you that no props, chicken-wire or otherwise, were involved."

Do you know?

SOLUTION ON PAGE 218

PALACES

It was a week or more after the final little lecture on memorising text verbatim that Holmes unfolded his pièce de résistance. Once again, I will give you what he said as exactly as I can.

There is one final memory technique that I want to share with you, Watson. It builds on everything I have shared with you so far. I was lucky to come to this technique early in my youth, thanks to Mycroft's generous training, and I assure you that it is the foundation of my abilities in observation. It is called the Memory Palace.

The principle is simple: you construct an imaginary environment within your mind, and use it as a system of storage within which data may be filed. I refer to these environments as wings. Each wing starts with a lobby, themed fancifully around the category of data it specialises in. A number of hallways stretch off from that lobby as necessary, representing subdivisions of the data and again themed accordingly, and then there are rooms off each hallway, for precise classification. Each room is decorated

with a number of loci according to need – from one pedestal in the centre to as many as nine unique placements on each wall, the ceiling, and the floor. Each locus is, of course, redolent of the datum you will hang there.

To store information, you create a mnemonic image of that datum and put in the effort to associate it with the appropriate locus in the correct room. When you return to that room, and that locus, the mnemonic will be there.

As you get more practiced in association – and as your mind begins to accept that this is a facility you want it to provide – it gets much faster and easier to remember mnemonics of all sorts, I promise. It is exactly like training in athletic abilities in that regard.

So to give you an advanced example, if am observing the mud-spatter on the hem of a traveller's cloak, I recall the transport wing, and the soilings hallway, and the spatter room, and the cabinet of mud patterns, and within that cabinet, I find the correct pattern linked to a note saying 'Hansom cab'.

Obviously, there is work to be done in setting up the initial wing. You should sketch out a simple map of the space, walk it repeatedly in your mind, break it into memorable loci, associate other senses with them, and so on. If you know you need an entire set of associations – and, my dear Watson, the Herigoné pegs from 00 to 99 do leap to mind – then you can prepare the entire environment in advance. In other cases, it might be more useful to just set up a small space, and expand later. Recall is, as always, the key.

Additionally, as you progress in this, the emphasis on your environments will convince your brain to make every aspect of this process quicker and easier, until it happens *almost* without your conscious volition. As your number of wings increases, and it will, the word 'Palace' will come into its own. In time, you will be able to walk the corridors of your palace from wing to wing – browsing the wonders you have stored within your mind.

103

PALACES 1

"Come, Watson," Holmes said. "Let us put word to action, and begin preparing a wing of your new memory palace within which to house the Herigoné pegs."

"Very well," I said. It was clear that resistance was futile, and as I've admitted elsewhere in these pages, I could see the utility of having the two-digit pegs committed to memory. I picked up my notepad and pencil.

"Capital. So, when you think of Herigoné pegs, what is the first image that comes to mind?"

"Numbers," I replied. "Lots of them."

Holmes nodded. "So your wing's lobby should be prodigiously decorated with numbers of various sizes and colours. I recommend two doors out of the lobby, undecorated ones to stand out, one of them a single door, for single digit pegs, and one a double door, for double-digit pegs."

"Very well," I said.

"I use a pair of rooms for each ten pegs, with 0, 1, 2, 3, and 4 imaged to loci placed left wall, front wall, right wall, ceiling and floor in one room, and 5, 6, 7, 8 and 9 in the same places in the other room. The connecting passage is in the front wall, to the side of the locus. You must of course feel free to adapt these suggestions to your own inclinations, my dear chap. Trust your intuition."

"That makes sense," I said. "I may change placements a little, but I will certainly keep them standard."

"It is for the best. For double-digit pegs, I have a hallway with doors opposite each other in pairs, marked 0 through 9. Through each door is another pair of rooms as before, containing the double-digit pegs beginning with the door's number. It is quite straightforward."

I nodded. "I see that."

"Excellent," Holmes said. "So you'll have no problem getting to on with construction of your new palace. The actual peg mnemonics will not come until after you have the wing vivid in your memory, after all. Remember – all five senses!"

I nodded and duly settled to work. With the benefit of hindsight as I write these words, I very much recommend you do the same.

First, without looking at any prompt, what is your passage from Julius Caesar?

SOLUTION ON PAGE 218

104

COINING

One day, I noticed that Holmes was idly performing tricks of legerdemain with a two-shilling piece, rolling it back and forth over the knuckles of one hand, spinning it in the air, and so on. He noticed my glance. "Coins can be the vehicle of all sorts of tomfoolery," he declared. "Sometimes usefully so."

"I'm quite sure," I said.

"So riddle me this. You are offered one of three coins in return for a true statement. One coin is copper, one is silver, and one is gold. The coin you are to receive is at the whim of the questioner. If your statement is not true, you will get no coin at all. We may assume that both you and your questioner wish to come away from this idiosyncratic transaction with the most money that the rules permit. Can you come up with the true statement that will guarantee you the gold coin?"

What do you think?

SOLUTION ON PAGE 219

105

LOAD

"Let us presume that I am of a mood to indulge in some landscape gardening," Holmes said while we were taking a little tea.

"I would not naturally presume any such thing," I protested. "You have never shown the least interest in such endeavours."

"Even so," he replied.

"Very well. What of it?"

"Simply this matter: is it easier to push a laden wheelbarrow or to pull it?"

Do you know?

SOLUTION ON PAGE 219

106

FOUL

"It was horrible, Mr. Holmes. Absolutely horrible." Rachel Green was a pleasant young woman of some substance, and it was clear that she had recently suffered a terrible shock.

Holmes nodded sympathetically.

"It was just Friday afternoon. Such a regular time of day. You never imagine... I looked through the drawing room window, and saw a woman being murdered. At Weychester Chase! Murdered! I could see the killer was a man, but neither he nor his... his victim were facing me, and the distance did not permit me to make any identifications. I'm afraid that I fled, and that has absolutely haunted me since. I'm no physical match for a murderer, but I would have called for help from one of the staff, or even gone to the telephone to raise assistance, truly I would. It was impossible."

The fact is that Miss Green's lack of intervention was, truly, not a matter of panicked cowardice, but of unfortunate circumstance.

Are you able to guess why?

SOLUTION ON PAGE 219

DARK

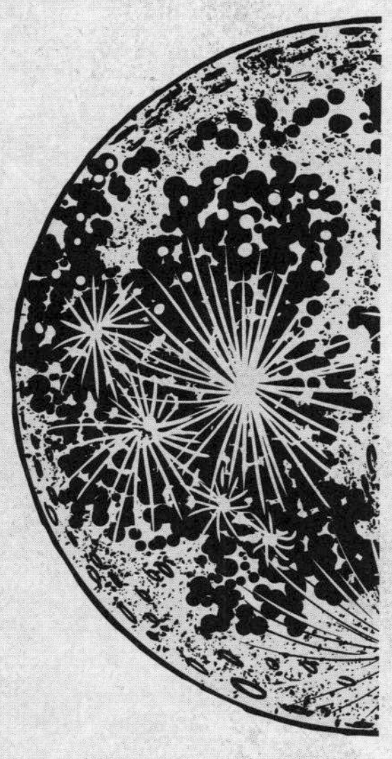

One of the side-effects of our occasional forays into the country is that Holmes's little mental challenges to me take on a distinctly pastoral air for a while. We'd been to Hookland for a couple of days during the Spitstone Bakery Affair, and the effects lingered for a good week afterwards.

I was shaking the afternoon rain off my hat, having just returned to 221b, when Holmes materialised by my side and said something about the moon. I apologised for not catching his comment, and asked him to repeat it.

"I said that I trusted you had noticed that we only ever see one side of the moon."

"Ah. Your trust is well-placed, old chap."

Holmes nodded at that. "The inescapable conclusion is that the moon rotates around the Earth at the precise rate that it rotates upon its own axis, a perfect one to one equivalence. If it were otherwise, we would see other areas of the moon at various times."

I thought about it and agreed that this did seem reasonable.

"In that case, I'm confident that you will be able to tell me whether this phenomenon is coincidental or not."

Alas, his confidence took a while to bear fruit.

What do you think?

SOLUTION ON PAGE 220

TESTAMENTAL

I have mentioned elsewhere that the great bulk of the late and not especially lamented Lord Culpepper's estate went to bedevil his sons, but there were other bequests, and most also had scorpioid stings in their tails.

Three of his old school chums were to be allowed to pick one artwork from the guest wing of the house. While the wing held a number of quality decorative items, one was more valuable than the rest. Fortunately, perhaps, the order in which the three were to be permitted their selection was provided for in the will as follows:

(a) No-one who has eaten lobster with me in Southampton is to choose before Nutty.

(b) If Stinker did not visit Cirencester eight years ago, the person to choose first never golfed with me on the first Thursday of the month.

(c) If second choice is between Stinker and Wilkins, Wilkins is to go before the one who first grew a beard.

Unfortunately, no-one concerned remembered any of the pertinent facts. Holmes pointed out that the rules would probably not have been chosen if they did not lead to a definitive solution, and that we should assume that at least two of the three statements had a role to play in deciding the order. Naturally, it then fell to me to find that solution which, eventually, I did.

Can you do it?

LAST WILL & TESTAMENT

SOLUTION ON PAGE 220

FIVES

"Would you do something for me, old friend?"

I looked up instantly. "Anything, Holmes. You know that."

"Capital. You are aware of the three different methods to find an average of a list of numbers?"

I boggled for a moment, then thought back to my epidemiology. "I remember that the mean is the average where you sum each number and divide by the number of items in the list. Ah... The median is the one that appears in the mid-point of the list if you write the numbers in order, I think?"

"It is," Holmes said. "There is also the mode, which is simply the most common of the numbers in the list. Another associated mathematical conceit is the range of the average, which is the difference between the highest and lowest items in the list."

"That sounds familiar," I admitted.

"Good. There are two lists of positive integers containing 5 numbers whose mean, median, mode, and range are all precisely 5."

"Are there, by God?" I muttered. "I suppose you'd like me to calculate them?"

"If you'd be so kind," he replied.

Can you figure out the two sets of numbers?

SOLUTION ON PAGE 221

CHILDREN

Mrs. Hudson was clearing away the things from breakfast, and I thought I perceived a degree of fatigue in her step that was far from typical. "My dear lady," I said to her, "pray forgive me any intrusion, but are you quite well? If there is any discomfort bothering you, I may have a remedy somewhere."

"Bless you, Doctor. It was just a busy evening yesterday. I was helping my Sally with a party. Four families of kids run you around a lot."

"I can imagine," I said. "How many were you dealing with?"

Her eyes lit up. "Well, as to that. There were fewer than eighteen in total, each family with a different number of children, and the interesting thing is that if you were to multiply each family's total of children together with the others, you'd get my Sally's street number."

"Ah."

"I know you're a clever man, Doctor. I haven't told you how many children there are in the smallest family – but now that I've spelled that lack out to you, I don't actually need to tell you. So why don't you tell me how many children the four families have?"

They say no good deed goes unpunished, so I endeavoured to answer the question.

Can you calculate the answer?

SOLUTION ON PAGE 222

EMERSON

Moving Forwards

Holmes had one last little lecture for me on the matter of memory. I took his words to heart, and – naturally – he was not wrong. I will reproduce the entirety of his comments below as closely as I can.

You now have access to all of the important tools of memorization in the mnemonic arsenal, my dear Watson. There are other, more specific tricks. Turning a set of concepts or objects into an amusing mnemonic phrase for example, such as "Richard Of York Gave Battle In Vain" for the colours of the spectrum, or "Please Excuse My Dearest Aunt Susan" for the order of the mathematical operators. I encourage you to look further into the subject of mnemonics, for it is both broad and deep. But the material you have learned so far offers near-endless flexibility.

It should be obvious at this point that since the mind responds to areas you focus on, the more work you put into memory techniques in general, the more responsive your individual mnemonic efforts of all sorts will become. In fact, because you are training your mind to the idea that this is the correct way to deal with your memory, many of these processes will begin to happen without your conscious deliberation. The benefits that this offers should be clear.

Although I have dealt with them separately, there is little practical difference between a route of loci and a memory palace. The palace is not grounded in physical experience and is thus harder to get your mind to recall vividly, but as you work more with your memory, this factor will become less relevant.

You can, of course, blend the two. You can hang entire rooms off the loci along your route – or, indeed, entire palaces for that matter. You can also construct palaces that house a route, or a dozen different routes. Herigoné pegs can be incorporated as well, helping you number loci or palace wings. The only limit is your ingenuity.

Another possibility to bear in mind is changing the environment of an established route or palace in a notable way. This allows you to use the same prepared space multiple times. So long as one change can apply to all points in the environment – it is underwater, everything is made of diamond, all colours are a vivid green, you are oddly minuscule, and so on and so forth ad infinitum – then your mind will treat the space as if it were new.

Picking a change relevant to the content you are memorizing will make it easy to recall. I mentioned the transport wing of my mind palace before. That is entirely constructed of polished wood, and padded benches abound, so as to resemble the interior of a respectable carriage. Never be afraid to experiment.

Treat your memory well, Watson, and it will treat you well in return. That is the sum of the matter. The rest is up to you.

SECTION FIVE

ANSWERS

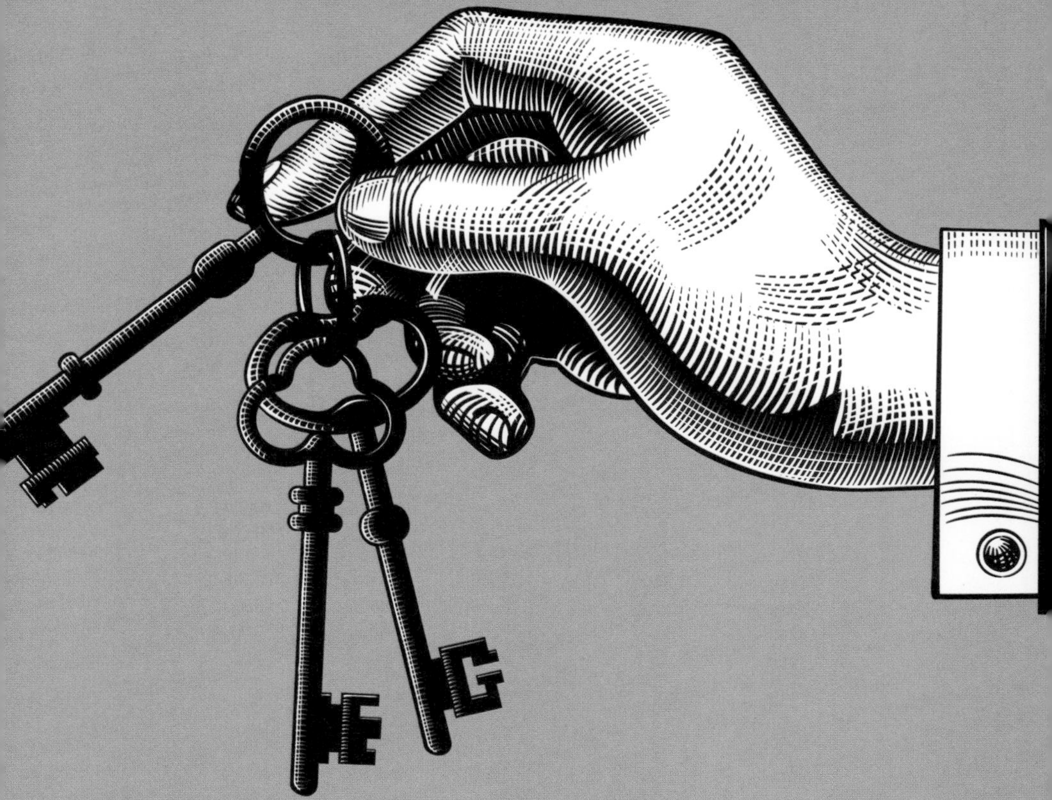

EASY

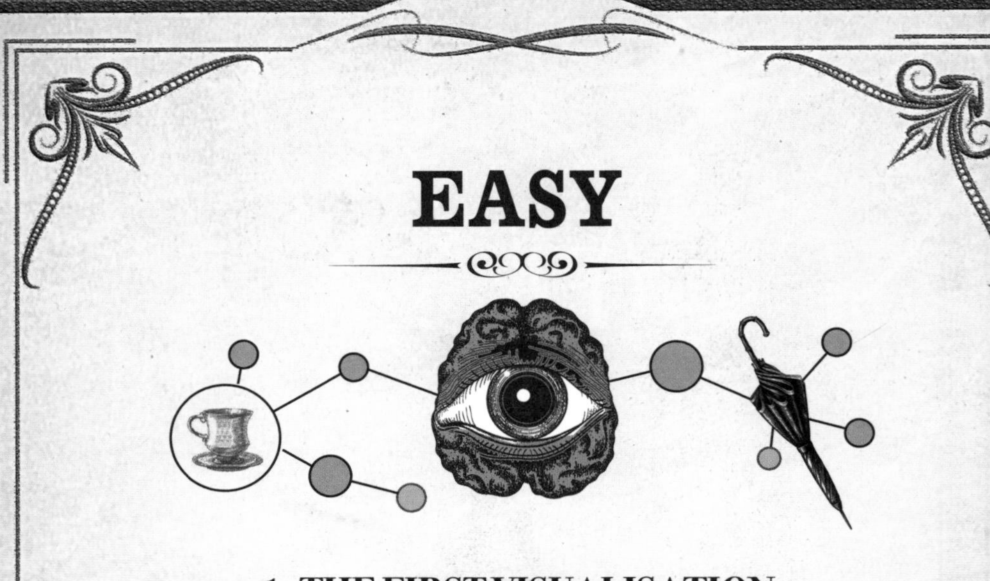

1. THE FIRST VISUALISATION

I picked an image of a quarter-pound block of butter on the butter dish that Mrs Hudson invariably makes use of. I trust you found something appropriately unexciting for yourself.

2. THE COLLECTOR

If nothing was correct in the article then he had neither fewer than nor more than 1,500 volumes, so he must have had exactly 1,500 volumes.

3. RAINBOW

The effect is only visible at the correct angle – specifically, when the line of the beam of light and the line of your vision both meet the mist or rain, the angle between the two lines must be 42 degrees. This also means the sun has to be behind you, so you are most likely to see rainbows in the east in evening, and in the west in the morning.

4. CROSSING

Not including the ship pulling in as you leave, you will pass fourteen other ships. One of these will be departing Manhattan as you arrive. You might think that with one ship a day, and a one-week journey, the answer would be seven, but you are seeing all the ships that left in the week before your departure, as well as all those that have left in the week since you departed. The inbound and outbound ships are both moving at the same speed towards each other. So you see one ship every 12 hours, not every 24.

5. MOUNTAIN TIME

While winds tend to be stronger at higher elevation, the primary reason for the drop in temperature is the thinning of the atmosphere. The effective air temperature varies according to the number of molecules of air hitting us (or the thermometer). The fewer air molecules, the fewer the collisions, and the lower the air temperature. The higher up you get, the thinner and colder the air gets.

6. FEATURED

In fact, most of our doubled organs serve important functions. Two eyes give us depth perception, two ears provide stereoscopic sound, and even two nostrils help us pinpoint the direction of a smell. It is all about locating the origin of the sensory input correctly. You can survive on one lung, but it makes exertion difficult. The primary exception lies with your kidneys. One healthy kidney is perfectly sufficient.

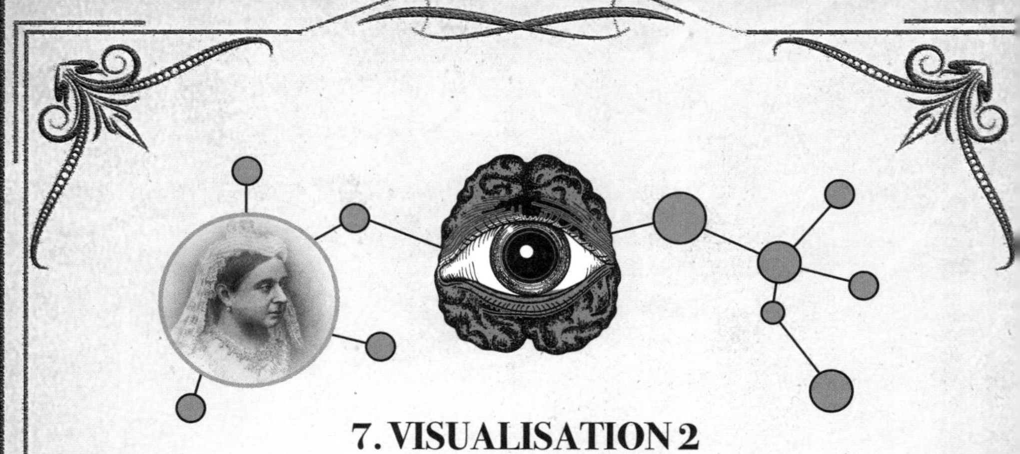

7. VISUALISATION 2

The thing Holmes asked me to recall last time was butter.

Holmes specifically forbade me from sharing my actual mnemonic images with you after the first, alas, but something just as absurd would be Her Majesty wearing a filthy coal-miner's lunch bucket on her head and aiming a golfing iron squarely at Isambard Kingdom Brunel's grimacing miniaturised head.

8. SECURITY CONCERNS

Each of the safe's three locks had two keys. Let us call them 1, 2, and 3. One partner kept the keys for locks 1 and 2, one for 1 and 3, and the third for 2 and 3. So, between them, any possible pairing would have keys for all three locks. Holmes solved the mystery when he demonstrated that the entire floor of the safe (and the floor beneath it) had been cut out from below, and replaced with identical, unharmed panels fashioned so cleverly as to appear pristine. The culprit turned out to be an assistant to the safe's creator.

9. EDNA

We have two facts. If Mrs Hudson's age is x now, then Edna's is $4x$. Additionally, formalising the situation five years ago, Mrs Hudson was aged $x-5$, and Edna was aged $5(x-5)$. Now, using Edna's current age as a starting point, five years ago her age would also have been expressible as $4x-5$. So $4x-5 = 5(x-5)$ or, expanding out the second term to get rid of the brackets,

4x-5 = 5x-25. We can add 25 to each side, so that 4x+20 = 5x, and then subtract 4x from each side to give us 20 = x. Since x is Mrs Hudson's age, she must be 20. Given that at least three of her daughters have children of their own, I cannot, in good faith, take this claim at face value.

10. THE WANDER

The fellow lived in Spitsbergen, deep in the Arctic Circle. The winter night there lasts for three months, and rather than spend all that time in the dark, he apparently went to spend some time with friends on the Norwegian mainland.

11. CLOCK, WISE

The invention of the clock was inspired directly by the existence of sundials. The hands of the clock represent the sun's shadow cast by the gnomon onto the plate. The Earth rotates anti-clockwise, so in the northern hemisphere, the shadow of the gnomon moves clockwise around the sundial. Since the clock was invented in thirteenth-century Europe, its makers copied the movement of the sundial in this hemisphere, after which everyone else copied the originals.

12. SHANE

Four, two boys and two girls. If there is one child, that child has to have a brother and a sister, so there is at least one child of each gender. But if there is a boy, he has to have a brother, and if there is a girl, she has to have a sister. So four is the minimum.

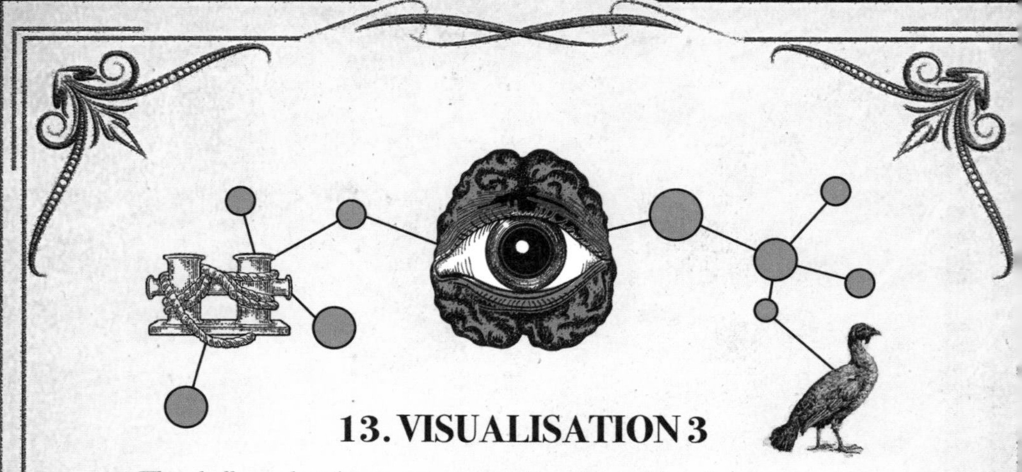

13. VISUALISATION 3

The challenge last time was to remember Queen Victoria.

I am permitted to reveal that my image was loosely based upon a certain memorable encounter I had with a charming Glaswegian patient, but my second thought about a prospective mnemonic was that Glasgow sounded just a little like "Glass Cow", and it does not seem difficult to imagine all sorts of curious images that could use a glass cow as a base.

14. STRAIGHT ACROSS

It is true for symmetrical shapes, but not for asymmetrical ones.

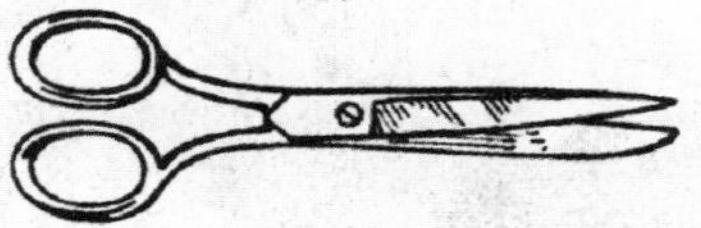

15. FLAGSTAFF

The cause is something called Bernoulli's principle, after an eighteenth century Swiss mathematician, and it can be most simply stated as, "As a fluid or gas speeds up, its pressure decreases." Even the slightest imperfections in a flag cause minute changes in the distance the air has to travel across its surface.

Since the air going over the imperfection is being forced along by all the air behind it, it has to speed up slightly to travel the extra distance. This decreases the pressure it exerts as it crosses that side of the fabric.

That produces a pressure imbalance between air on the two sides of the flag, and being pliable, the flag is pushed slightly outwards on the lower-pressure side. This, in turn, produces a greater obstacle to the air, and the effect intensifies, until the air flowing around the flag becomes unpredictably turbulent. Thus the flag waves and ripples around. If a flag was somehow treated to become rigid enough to resist the small differences in air pressure, it would behave – and look – like a colourful weather vane.

16. LYNN

The poor fellow had not been hung by the neck, but by the harness of the parachute he had been wearing, and it was the cold night that had killed him. The air balloon he had been riding in was found a couple of fields away, the basket broken by the force of its crash-landing. The police thought that the balloon itself had caught fire. The balloonist had attempted to leap to safety, but he'd been unable to extricate himself from the tangle he'd landed in, and the weather had claimed his life.

17. COLD

The frustrating truth is that we just don't know why influenza – or the common cold, for that matter – are seasonal. One possibility is that people are more likely to socialise indoors during winter (or monsoon season) than they are at other times. Being in a confined space does make it easier for the disease to pass from one person to another than if they are outdoors, in the fresh air. But that is just a theory. The disease itself is not critically dependent on temperature or air moisture for its transmission, as its tropical behaviour shows.

18. TRIBALITY

Only Right can tell you something correct, and if Bill was Right, he could not describe himself as Wrong, so Bill has to be Wrong. Because he is Wrong, his statement must be incorrect, and so both men cannot be Wrong. Thus, Mick has to be Right.

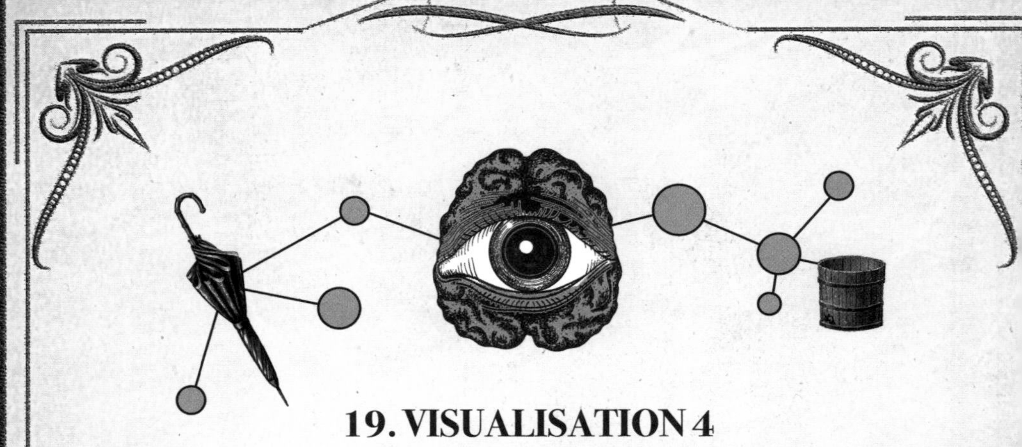

19. VISUALISATION 4

Last time, I asked you to recall the city of Glasgow.

By this point, I trust you are sufficiently practised to be able to come up with some sort of charged reminder for rain which is, after all, a fundamental part of life in most of Europe. Mine was, I admit, positively risqué, and I begin to understand Holmes's insistence that I do not share my personal mnemonics with anyone.

20. LUNACY

Although the visible crescent moon is the only portion of the new moon directly illuminated by the sun, the rest of its face does receive some of the sun's light scattered back to it from Earth, thus being very faintly visible.

21. WATERY CAN

The second effect is straightforward. Water has a fairly high surface tension, and the strength of that is more than sufficient to keep the streamlets together. This is the same quality that allows you to (cautiously) overfill a glass with water so that there is a noticeable bump on top.

The first effect is only slightly trickier, but it is less intuitive. Water's pressure to escape from a hole comes from the height – not the volume, just the height – of the water above the hole. Simplifying slightly, this is because only the water directly above the pressure point is being pulled down onto it by gravity. At ground level, the atmosphere exerts approximately the same pressure of a column of water thirty feet tall. So unless the holes are big enough for air to press in on the water inside, the pressure of the water in your can is unable to compete.

Were it possible to empty your can of all contents, air included, the apparent resistance you would feel to opening it would not directly be the vacuum inside, but the difference of pressure between the inside (none) and the atmosphere around you – around fourteen and a half pounds of force per square inch at sea level. Vacuum does not exert pressure. All the work is done by gravity.

22. BISCUITRY

If Lestrade had both three times as many biscuits as I, and also eight more, then eight is the difference between my number of biscuits and three times that amount, and thus is twice my number. Half of eight is four. I supposedly had four biscuits – although I must protest here – and so Lestrade had twelve, and Holmes had two.

23. METEORIC

With Holmes's gentle assistance, I got there in the end. A meteorite significant enough to leave a crater impacts the Earth with incredible force, and this is so large as to completely overwhelm any effects associated with its direction of travel or the peculiarities of its shape. Effectively, it acts like a bomb, even if coming from a very shallow angle.

24. A DISPLACEMENT

The remaining ball will be white two times out of three, for a probability of 66.6%. Although only two balls were ever in the pouch, since you don't know the starting condition, there are still three possible ways to draw two balls out that start with a white ball – New White followed by Original White, Original White followed by New White, and New White followed by Original Black. Each of the three is equally likely, so in 2/3rds of cases, you will draw a second white ball from the pouch.

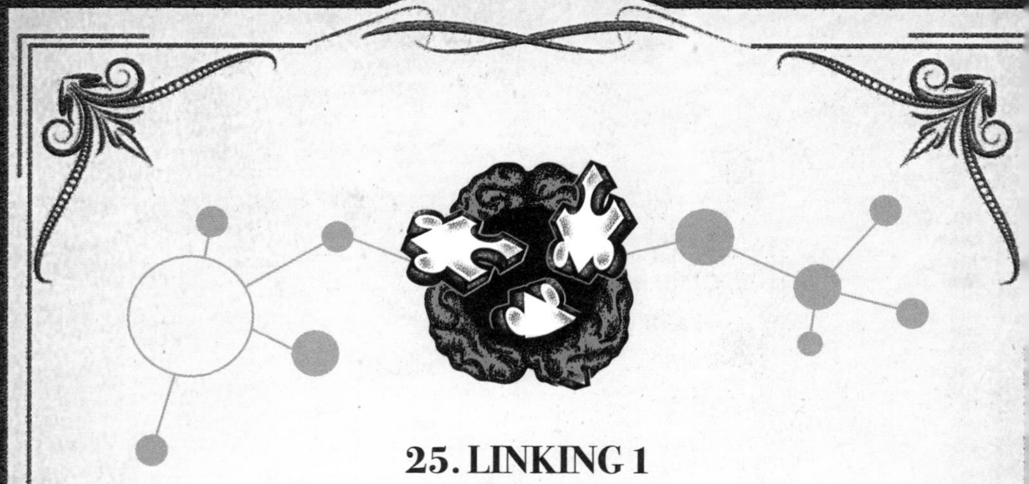

25. LINKING 1

The last mnemonic I asked you to remember was rain.

Memorising the chain of linked mnemonics for the menswear felt odd, and a little alien, but after a number of successful repetitions, I was able to recall the list with reasonable fluidity. My images were deeply absurd, of course.

26. THE LURCHER

Grey, Holmes informed me, had a curious horror about stepping onto the gaps between pavement slabs. On the macadam roadway, and in the grassy park, there were no cracks to disturb him. It must have been an exhausting problem to have.

27. TRIO

Arthur is the left-most individual, as both Barry and Colin are to his right. But it is not possible to say which of the latter two is where.

28. DARKNESS

The Moon does not stay in exactly the same plane as it orbits us, but moves up and down. Sometimes it is too far above the direct line between the Earth and the Sun to cast a shadow onto the Earth, and sometimes too far below.

29. CULPEPPER

If the first man is the murderer, he is lying about the second man, which would provide two murderers, which we know is not the case. So he must be telling the truth. Because he is telling the truth, the second man is innocent and must also be telling the truth. None of the three suspects are guilty.

30. SHIPSHAPE

Since they returned at the same time, the journeys took the same time. However, they will have experienced different numbers of sunrises. The ship heading west would have stretched its days a little so as to experience one less apparent day than passed back in Tasmania, and by the opposite principle, the ship heading east would have shortened its days slightly to experience one more. This discrepancy was eventually alleviated with the establishment of the Greenwich Prime Meridian as the dominant global measure of zero degrees longitude in 1884, with the de facto international date line running on the opposite side of the world to the Meridian.

MEDIUM

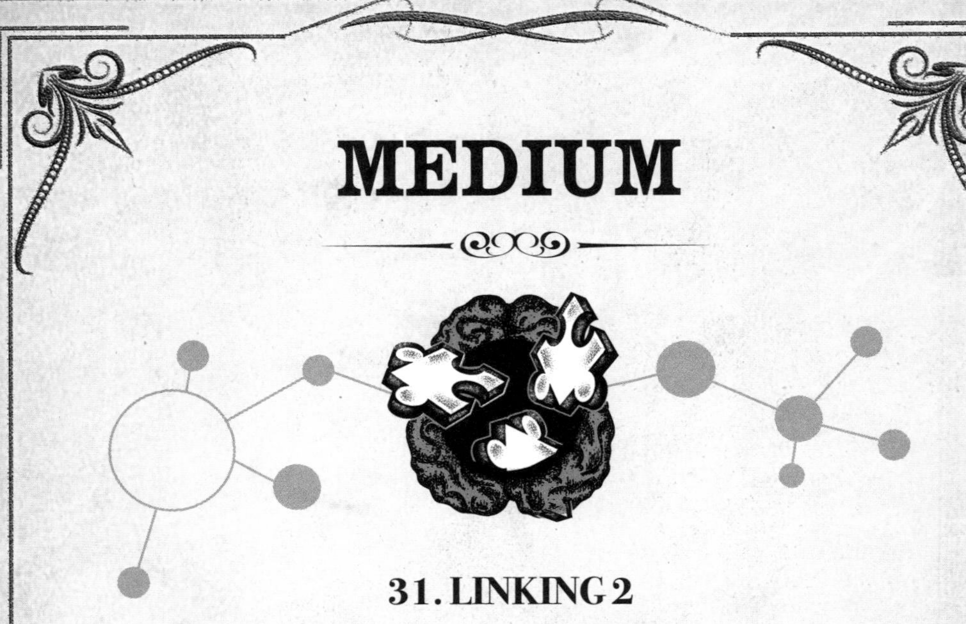

31. LINKING 2

The first chain was items of menswear comprising a top hat, a jacket, a bow tie, gloves and a pair of calf-high boots.

32. RULE

It should be obvious that the "A" card needs to be checked to see if its number is odd. But there is one more card to flip, and I picked the wrong one. "No, Watson," Holmes told me. "An easy slip, but if the [1] card has a vowel on the other side, it is compliant, and if it has a consonant, the rule does not apply. There is no possibility of it breaking the rule. But the [2] card does need to be examined, for while it cannot be in compliance with the rule, if it has a vowel on the hidden side, then it is breaking the rule."

33. FÖHN

The Föhn can form in the lee shadow of a mountain. As air at normal ambient temperature and moisture is blown over the mountain, its pressure drops because of the elevation, and the air cools. The cooler it is, the less moisture it can hold, and it drops most of its water vapour as snow or rain. On its descent on the other side of the mountain, the air is recompressed, and its temperature rises, but because the air has lost its moisture, it cannot normalise its temperature easily through internal evaporation. So it becomes a hot, dry wind. In addition to this, some atmospheric mixing at the turbulent mountaintop – or sometimes even prevailing pressure – draws higher, drier winds down the mountain, which take on the same characteristic for the same reasons.

34. GARLIC NUTS

The correct technique for this unlikely situation, according to Holmes, is to place a lone ginger nut in one jar, and all the other biscuits in the other jar. That way, if your single-biscuit jar is selected, you are guaranteed a good result, while if the other jar is selected, you still have a 49/99 chance of getting the right biscuit. So the total odds of getting a true ginger nut are just a little under 75% (74.75%, to be exact). To my mind, the better solution is to implore Mrs Hudson to excuse us from garlic-flavoured biscuits.

35. LIARS

If Ted is telling the truth, then Adam is lying about Matthew, which means Matthew is also telling the truth – which would make Ted a liar. That is contradictory, so Ted is lying, and Adam is telling the truth. Adam says Matthew is lying, and indeed he claims that the other two are lying. Therefore the correct pattern is that Adam is telling the truth while Ted and Matthew are both lying. If only the real trio had been so transparent.

36. MOST FOUL

The arresting officer had overlooked the fact that Wilkins's coat was designed to be reversible. At some point during the morning, he had been splashed with mud, and had turned his coat inside out, moving the cosh from left to inside right.

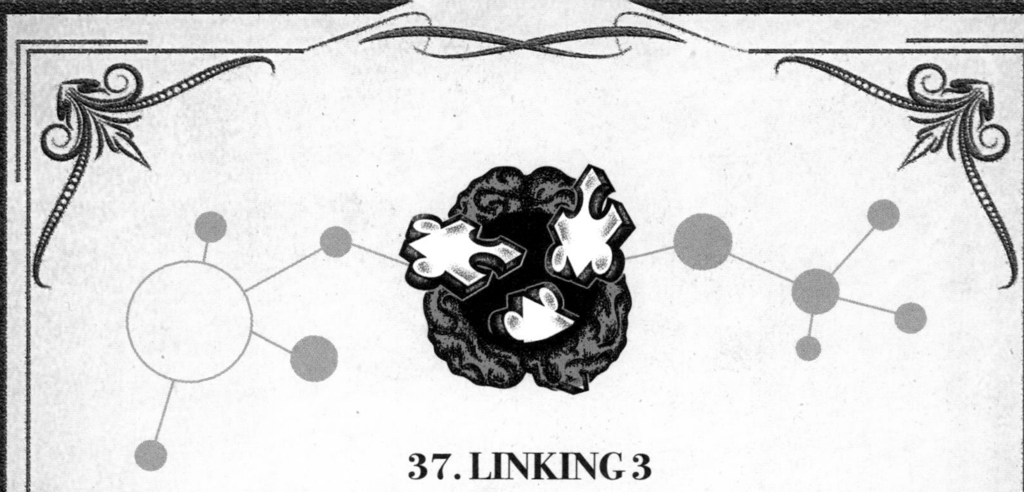

37. LINKING 3

The previous list was of foodstuffs – a jar of honey, an apple, two fried eggs, a cucumber, a loaf of bread and a cup of piping hot tea. It took me a moment or two to secure my initial mnemonic image, which involved a swarm of bees and some unlikely apian antics, but once I had that, the rest of the items came quite simply.

38. ROULETTE

According to Holmes, gambling with purloined wealth is an excellent way to make the money much harder to subsequently locate. The casino unwittingly gets your stolen money in various forms, and pays out your winnings using utterly innocuous banknotes, bearer bonds, or house chips. Roulette is apparently a frequent choice because the technique is trivially easy and if you cover both sides of an outside bet, your overall loss will be less than 3%. You can do better than that on certain other games, but not without significant skill.

39. TRANSPARENT

Wet frosted glass. The water evens out some of the frosting, making it more transparent. Drying it off with a clean cloth restores its opacity.

40. COLD SNAP

The rub is that there has to be moisture in the air in order for snowfall to occur. Very cold air holds almost no moisture. In temperate climes, an air temperature much below -15 degrees centigrade means that the air is unlikely to hold enough water for a snowfall. The polar regions are, in fact, technically arid deserts, with less than ten inches of precipitation a year, mostly in spring and autumn. They remain extremely snowy because of gradual build-up and very restricted melting. Were some calamity to warm the Earth's climate even a degree or two, they would start losing their snow and ice.

41. FALLS

I was not, in fact, totally wrong. The scream will fade in volume. But apparently, as the unlucky victim accelerates under the effects of gravity, the pitch will also change. The faster he becomes, the deeper his scream will sound. This effect is named for an Austrian physicist, Christian Doppler.

42. ONE APPLE

Holmes swiftly demolished my answer. "I'm sure you'll agree that one third is 0.333... recurring, and that three thirds are 1. Since three times 0.333... is 0.999... then 0.999... recurring has to be equal to 1. As it indeed is. Mathematics does curious things when infinity becomes involved, old chap."

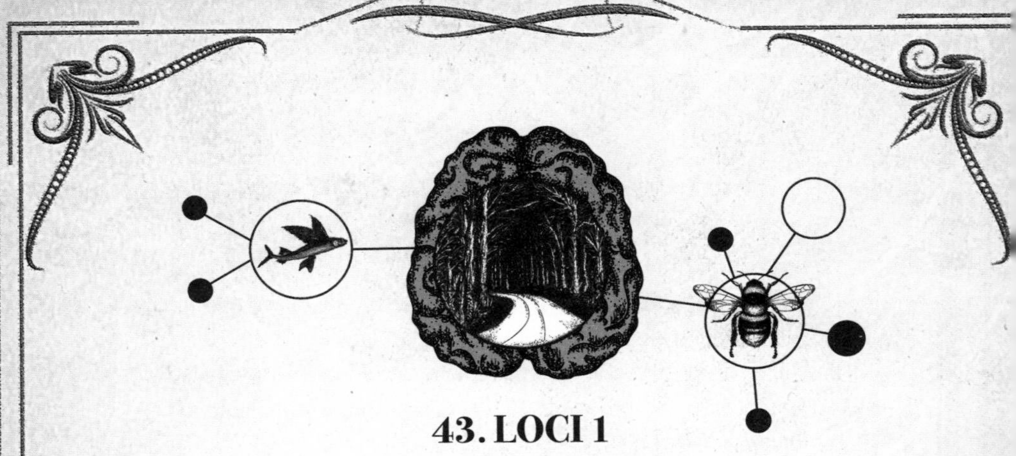

43. LOCI 1

Finding the initial item in the list was, once again, a bit of a challenge. I immediately saw the advantage that starting with a specific locus to prompt oneself would provide. Holmes's list was of things he considered needful, and consisted of a pipe, a newspaper, a book, a grandfather clock, a magnifying glass, a medical syringe and a box of matches.

44. TERMINUS

The man killed himself. It came out that he was gravely ill, and Holmes was certain that rather than drag out a painful death – and make his wife suffer through having to care for him – he took his own life in a manner that suggested murder, so as to spare her from any shame or guilt. He further speculated that a life assurance policy might also be involved, one which would be voided by suicide.

45. SOLAR

First, let us recall Mr Newton. The Earth does not fall into the Sun because it is moving too quickly. If the Sun vanished out of existence, the Earth would move away in a straight line, perpendicular to the circle of its orbit of where the Sun had been. But the Sun is still in place, fortunately, and the element of that velocity that would take the planet further from the Sun's location is precisely equalled by the pull of the Sun. So we are in a perfectly stable loop, like every other one of the Sun's satellites. Which is why we do not get pulled in.

The Moon does not get pulled away from us for exactly the same reason. It is circling the Sun in an orbit that precisely matches our own. Earth's presence and greater size also pull it around us, and because we are a self-interested species we tend to think that this is the more important, but our pull on the Moon is less than half as much as the Sun's – sufficient to keep it rotating around us, but when all is said and done, the Moon orbits the Sun first, and us second.

46. TONE

"It is a simple matter, my dear Watson. The tone is coming from the fence behind him. Each fencepost has its own small echo, and the regular spacing of the posts means that the thump is echoed back from each of them in a series of regular intervals. This fractures the resulting sound, and causes the ringing tone."

47. SENTENCE

If Spare was 24 and the guard 52, the guard was 28 years older than he was. So when Spare was 28, he would be half the guard's age, and would be released.

48. TARGET

You would need to aim to the left. This is known as the Coriolis Effect after Gaspard-Gustave de Coriolis, who described it mathematically some decades ago. It occurs because of conservation of momentum, and is best explained over global scales. At the equator, the Earth is spinning clockwise at over 1000 miles an hour. At the exact poles, it is not spinning at all. If you fire your bullet straight north from the equator, it will also have to be moving 1000 miles an hour eastwards, otherwise it would immediately shoot off to the west. As the bullet progresses, it retains that eastward velocity, even though the planet beneath it is no longer moving so quickly. This corresponds into the bullet seeming to drift eastwards as its own eastward velocity starts to exceed that of the ground. In order to correct this eastward drift, you must aim westwards, or left. Note that this force applies in the opposite direction in the southern hemisphere, because the equator is the point of maximum speed around which it hinges. You can see the effects in the differing rotational directions of cyclones north and south of the equator, but on either side, this effect is why they form. The wind sweeping out from the equator moves faster than the planet, and so it is forced into a spin as it meets slower air.

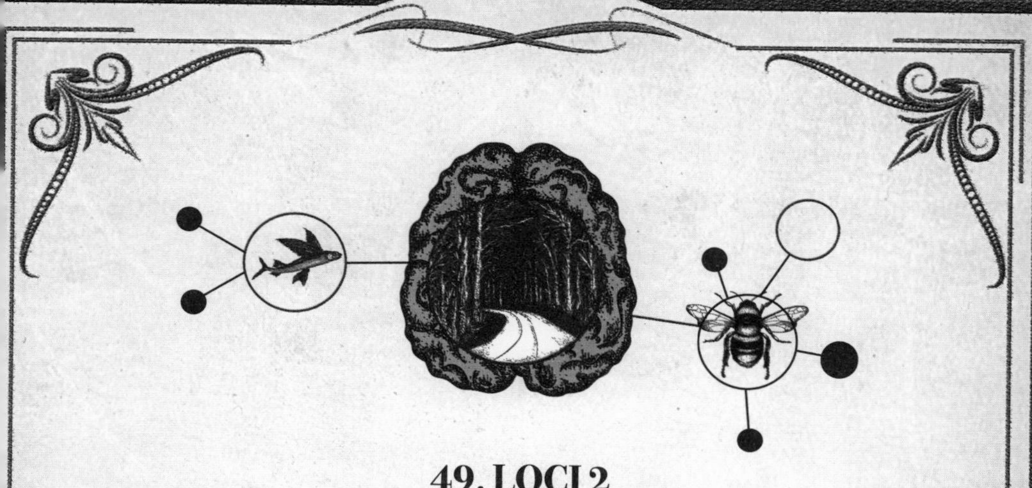

49. LOCI 2

Only you can know whether you have memorised your route of loci. But to help start you off with making mnemonics of Holmes's list, I will share the somewhat gruesome fact that I turned my memory of the exit from the train station into a ventricle of a beating heart, red and fleshy, filling with blood and then expelling me out onto the pavement in a gout that carries me to my next landmark. My guess is that you will settle on something less vividly medical.

50. NOTES

Only the statement: "Exactly one of these statements is true," is true. If none of them are true, then the "none" note would become true, falsifying it. If the "two" statement is true, then the "one" statement would be false, so there would be just one true statement, and the same logic applies to "three", "four", and "five". So exactly one of the statements is true.

51. TWINKLER

In short, it's too big. The Earth's atmosphere is volatile, with all sorts of small gusts and eddies and other disturbances appearing – and disappearing – all the time. These affect the passage of a beam of light, shifting it around ever so slightly. Stars, which appear as mere pinpricks, are thus constantly being minutely deflected, and seem to shimmer. The moon, however, is a much larger object, and the small deflections appearing to occur from point to point on its surface average out.

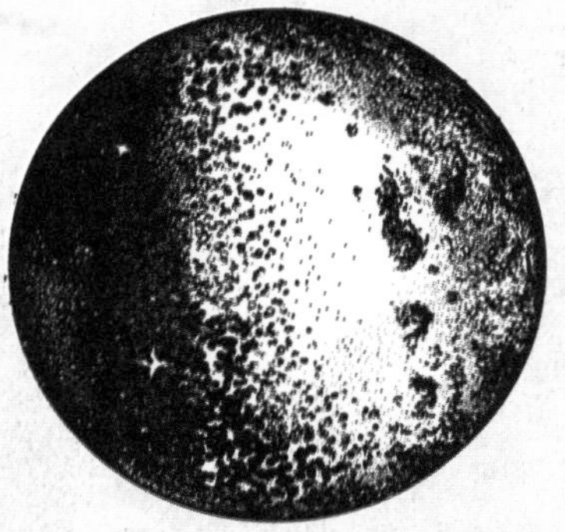

52. BUBBLE

The internal pressure is higher than that of the surrounding air. If the internal pressure were less than the atmospheric pressure, the bubble would instantly collapse. So we can rule that possibility out. When you make a soap bubble, you blow through a film that is caught in a hoop, stretching out the bubble until it breaks free. The fact that it is able to exist at all shows that the soap film has significant surface tension, and if you stop blowing before a bubble forms, the film will return to its flattened state. That force still exists when the film forms a bubble, and it is pushing inwards. Since the bubble does not collapse, the pressure of the air inside must be precisely sufficient to counteract the combined pressure of both the surface tension and the atmosphere. Thus it has to be higher than just the surrounding atmospheric pressure. In fact, during the formation process, the bubbles contract until the two sets of pressures perfectly balance.

53. CANE

Three times. If the cane is broken at random, then there will be two portions, one of which is smaller than or equal to the other. Now, note that the smaller piece can only have been separated at a point from the very edge through to the centre point of the cane. If it had been separated further that the centre, it would not be the smaller piece. Since each position along the length is equally likely when chosen at random, its length will average to the centre point of this possible range – one quarter of the way along the whole stick. Thus, on average, the smaller piece is one foot long, leaving three feet for the longer piece.

54. CULPABILITY

If the first man is guilty, he is lying about the second man's innocence, but that would mean two men were guilty, which we know not to be the case. So the first man is telling the truth. Since he is telling the truth, the second man is innocent and is also telling the truth. That makes the third man guilty, and Lestrade had his man at last.

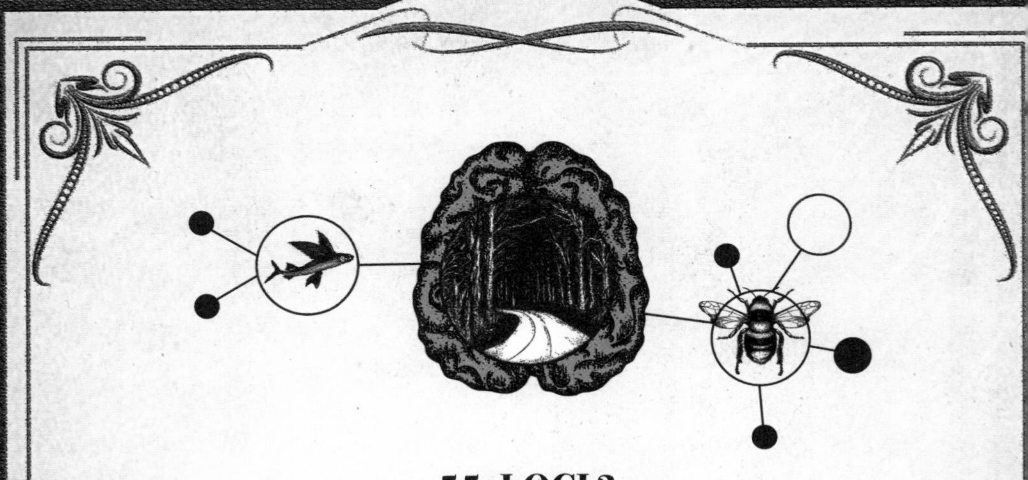

55. LOCI 3

The list was of imagery taken from recent novel titles, and consisted of a heart, five children, a white bird, a hotel, four feathers, the moon, a green shutter, a purple cloud, a boat and a brass bottle.

56. TRUEL

Worst should deliberately miss both men. If he happens to kill Medium, Good will certainly kill him. If he happens to kill Good, then Medium will have a strong chance of killing him. If he kills neither, Medium knows that he poses the greater threat to Good, and so will have to try to shoot him. If he succeeds, then it is Worst's turn again. If he misses, then Good, by the same reasoning, will kill Medium, and once again, it is Worst's turn. In either instance, by missing both, Worst leaves himself a situation where he is in a duel, and has first shot, while if he kills one of the other men, he is still in a duel, but has second shot against a more-skilled opponent.

Holmes did not discuss the particulars of the mathematics of the matter with me, but in case you were curious, he suggested that, in fact, Worst's chance of survival if he deliberately misses his first shot is 40%, compared to Medium's 38%, and Good's 22%. By comparison, if he kills Medium, his chance of survival is a guaranteed 0%, and if he kills Good, it is still only 14%.

57. SALARY

The first added an unspecified sum to his salary, and told the second. The second added his own correct salary, and told the new figure to the third. The third then added his salary in turn, and told the total to the first. The first then subtracted his unspecified sum to get the accurate combined total of their salaries, and divided this by three to share the average with the other two.

58. RECOLLECT

No. Twenty-four hours afterwards, it would have been 1:32am again, so bright sunshine would not have been possible.

59. CRIME

It is suicide. Failed attempts are punished harshly to dissuade others, rightly or wrongly, but the dead are beyond prosecution. Personally, I think the policy is cruel and incorrect, and Scots law agrees with me, but there you have it. It is my hope that in a more enlightened age, parliament will see fit to change the law, and stop committing further harm to those in need.

60. CENTURY

If you go second, you always pick the number which, when added to the first man's number, totals eleven. If he picks 2, you pick 9; if he picks 7, you pick 4. This will bring the total to 99 after your ninth turn, making it inevitable that he will lose. The only counter-strategy if going first is to hope that the second man fails to total to a multiple of eleven, which then gives you the chance to take the initiative of getting to a multiple of eleven going forward.

TRICKY

61. HÉRIGONE 1

I came up with train, animal, renter, liniment, and terminal. I am certain there are other possibilities equally as good.

62. MIRROR MIRROR

As Holmes eventually pointed out to me, the mirror does not reverse your reflection left to right, but rather front to back. It shows you precisely what you would see if you were standing in front of yourself looking at yourself. We think of it as a left-right transformation because we are used to looking out of our faces rather than at them. I, however, did manage to find the answer to the second part of the question myself – if you lie the mirror on the floor at your feet and look down into it, you will be vertically reflected.

63. AMELIA

It took me far longer than the cup of tea or the entire plate of macaroons, but I did get there in the end. The trick lies in knowing what you don't know and what that implies. So we know the three ages multiply to 36, and there's only a certain number of possibilities for that. But we are also told that adding them together does not produce a unique solution. So let's look at the possibilities.

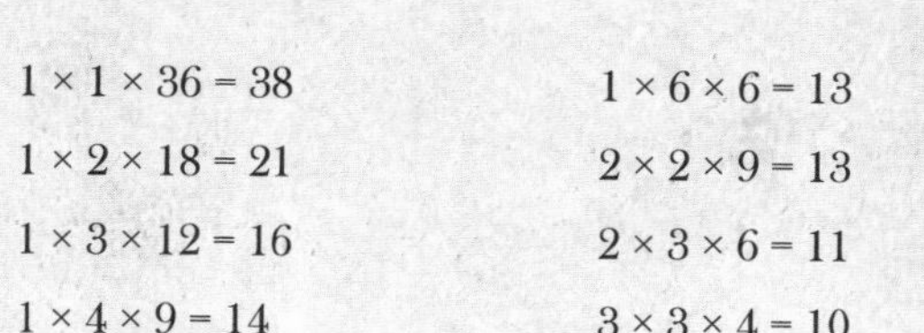

$1 \times 1 \times 36 = 38$

$1 \times 2 \times 18 = 21$

$1 \times 3 \times 12 = 16$

$1 \times 4 \times 9 = 14$

$1 \times 6 \times 6 = 13$

$2 \times 2 \times 9 = 13$

$2 \times 3 \times 6 = 11$

$3 \times 3 \times 4 = 10$

Of these options, the only sum that is not unique is 13. So Amelia lives at Number 13, and her children are either 1, 6 and 6, or 2, 2 and 9.

Now, we're told that Alexander's age makes the question answerable. That means his age has to rule one of the possibilities out, but not the other. If he were 10 or more, it wouldn't do so, and if he were 6 or less, he wouldn't be older than either possibility. So Amelia's children are 1, 6 and 6, and Alexander has to be 7, 8 or 9. Of those, only 8 is an even number. Therefore, Alexander is 8.

64. WORKERS

Once I remembered that Australia was a celebrated location for pearl fishing, the situation made sense. The men were pearl fishers, working deep underwater, and were menaced by sharks. The one who panicked shot to the surface, gave himself decompression sickness, and died. The one who took his time to surface safely had to keep the sharks at bay, and received several bites, but survived without loss of limb.

65. PUB

According to Holmes, the men were members of a criminal syndicate. The leader had realised that one of the fellows was a turncoat, but didn't know which one. So he pre-arranged the delivery boy's arrival and told the rest that the identity of the traitor would be delivered to him any moment. As soon as the lad appeared, the actual traitor panicked and fled, marking himself out.

66. CHAMPAGNE

The fizz comes from carbon dioxide dissolved in the liquid. It takes a certain amount of energy for the gas to effervesce from the liquid, and because gas takes up more room than liquid, this means disturbing the liquid's surface. When you open the bottle gently, air pressure and the wine's own surface tension provide sufficient force to make it difficult for bubbles to form. However, if you have shaken the bottle, you have already created lots of tiny microbubbles in the liquid from the internal air mixing with it – and also disrupted the surface tension as those microbubbles form and then are reabsorbed – so the energy required for the carbon dioxide to effervesce is much smaller. The more bubbles there are breaking the surface, the easier it is for other bubbles to form, which is why a bottle will sometimes build to overflowing.

On top of that, on a molecule by molecule basis, by far the most energy is required for the initial bubble of gas to form. It is significantly easier for a bubble to grow from added gas than it is for the bubble to first appear out of the liquid.

As observable tests of effervescence, you'll find: cold champagne is less effervescent than warm because the liquid holds less energy; higher air pressure makes it far less effervescent than normal, and low air pressure because of the extra force on the liquid's surface; if you tipped in some salt or sugar all those extra surfaces to effervesce onto would create a surge of bubbles; and that if you shook a bottle that somehow had no air whatsoever in it, it would be much less fizzy when you opened it, because there would be less internal turbulence and far fewer microbubbles to provide initial seeding.

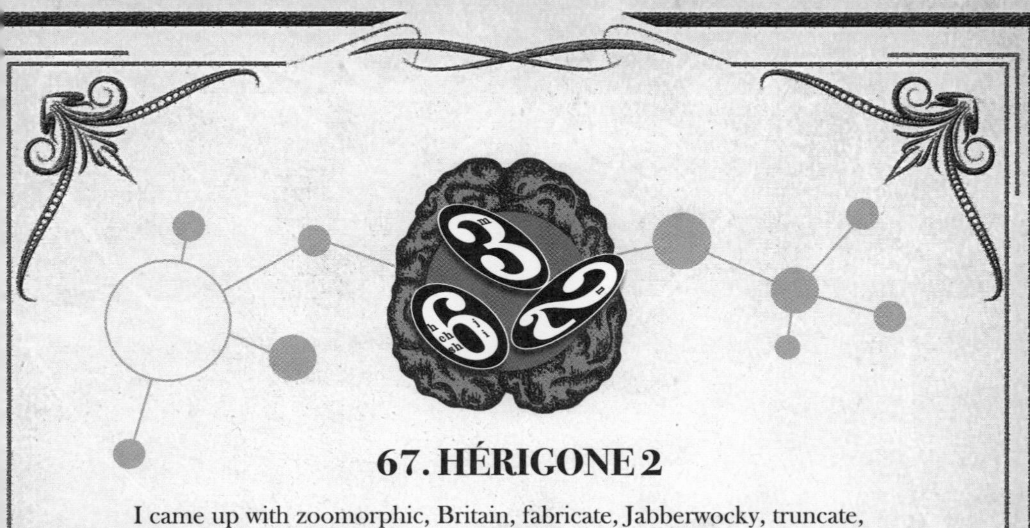

67. HÉRIGONE 2

I came up with zoomorphic, Britain, fabricate, Jabberwocky, truncate, and cross-cut. Holmes appeared to find these choices idiosyncratic, by which I assume that there are plenty of solid alternatives for at least some of the numbers.

68. BRINY

It turns out that because of differences in the freezing points of water and brine, and their relative densities, the brine descends through the ice over time, pulled by gravity. After a year or so, sea-ice is drinkable, if still a bit brackish, and after several years it is almost completely salt-free. I flatly refuse to consider the implication that there is a city of cruel fish-people lurking under the Arctic ice, however.

69. RULERSHIP

It is a matter of friction. The friction between finger and ruler depends on the exact location of the finger along the ruler's length, as well as minuscule variations in the skin of your fingers, the angles they are at, and so on. The closer your finger is to the centre of the ruler, the greater the weight on it. Unless the frictions are identical – which will only happen in the instant that the weight on the two fingers is balanced – the ruler will slide only on the point of lesser resistance.

70. STARRY

After a period of thought – and, I confess, a very brief nap – I came up with several possible answers. Firstly, some of these stars must be a mind-bendingly great distance away, so not all of their light will have necessarily arrived at us yet. Secondly, stars are not eternal, so they are not all alight at the same time, and indeed perhaps they die at a swifter rate than they are born. Thirdly, perhaps the stars are not evenly distributed, but clumped – after all, looking into the heart of the Milky Way, the night sky does seem white in places. Fourthly, there could be something blocking some of the light that either will simply not heat to radiance in time, or has not yet had sufficient opportunity to do so. Fifthly, perhaps the universe is not in fact infinite after all, or at least perhaps the matter within it simply runs out after a while. Finally, the light we can see is only a small part of the electromagnetic spectrum, and perhaps not all starlight is visible – it could be that if we could see a greater range of energies, the night sky would look white.

71. SPHERE

The answer, of course, is gravity. Over an extended period of time, the matter that makes up the Earth will be pulled into the most gravitationally stable form – a sphere. Continental drift creates mountains of course, but they are insignificant. Even mighty Everest represents a deviation of little more than a tenth of one per cent of the planet's radius. Our rotation does try to fling the equator out a little, but the best it can do is a flattening of less than one per cent of the Earth's radius.

72. SAND ON THE BEACH

The weight of your body disturbs the sand under and around your foot. Sand is pushed down beneath you, but is also forced out away from your sole. This makes the sand around the edge of your foot rise up. The water, which soaks through sand thanks to capillary action, cannot move as quickly as the sand your weight is pushing up. So the raised sand is dry for a few moments, before the water catches up.

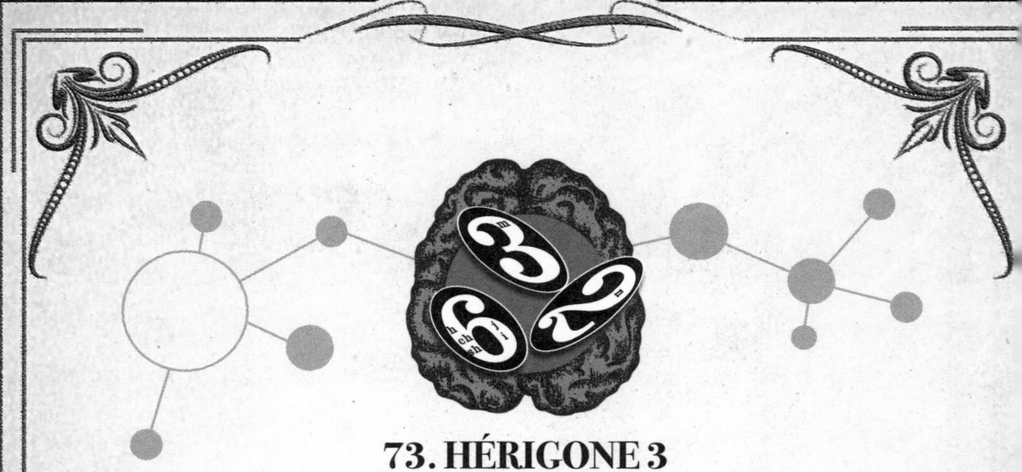

73. HÉRIGONE 3

Again, I'm sure there are better solutions, but I came up with keel for 75, knife for 28, rear for 44, jail for 65, fuzz for 80, name for 23, mob for 39 and bhaji, a style of Indian fritter, for 96.

74. CRACK THE CODE

We know that 7, 3, and 8 are not in the answer. Two of the three are in 780, and since one of those three digits is in the answer, the answer must contain – but not end in – 0. 206 has two digits of the answer in the wrong positions, so 0 cannot be in the middle either. The code starts with 0, and either 2 or 6 (but not both) are also in the answer. 645 and 682 both start with 6, and have respectively 1 incorrectly placed and 1 correctly placed digit. That digit cannot be 6, which is in the same place both times. So 2 is the other digit of 206 in the answer, and from 682, 2 goes at the end. Finally, from 645, we know either 4 or 5 is in the answer, but in the wrong position. Since the only uncertain spot left is the centre, and 4 is in the centre already, that must be wrong, and 5 has to be the middle digit. Thus 052 is the solution.

75. OWLS

The heart of the matter is that despite the complicated chain of events, the salesman completes two transactions, and the fact that it is the same object makes no actual difference. In one transaction, he buys for six and sells for seven. In the other, he buys for eight and sells for nine. So he makes one shilling each time, for a profit of two shillings. Or, mathematically speaking, his profit is 7+9 = 16, and his costs 6+8 = 14, and 16-14 = 2.

76. TIDE

Gravity gets stronger the closer the attracting body is. As the moon orbits the Earth, it pulls the surface of the planet towards itself a little. Water is far more mobile than rock, and so the water is pulled upwards towards the moon, generating a higher water level – a high tide – at the point nearest the moon. But at the same time, it is also pulling the whole Earth. The water furthest from the moon, on the other side of the planet, is pulled less than the planet is, and so it too forms a high tide, but this time the water level is higher because the planet is being pulled away beneath it.

77. FLY

Flies' feet are covered in swathes of very thin hairs that terminate in minuscule pads. These pads are so fine that the molecules that make them up and the molecules of the surface that they are touching electrically attract each other, an effect known as the van der Waals Force. It is extremely weak, but there are a great many pads on each foot, and in combination they are strong enough to support the insect.

78. APPLES

The poor fellow wasn't watching where he was going and he fell into a hole in the ground – an old well shaft, as it happened, and 80 feet deep. Apparently the cover had rotted through some years before, and he hadn't realised.

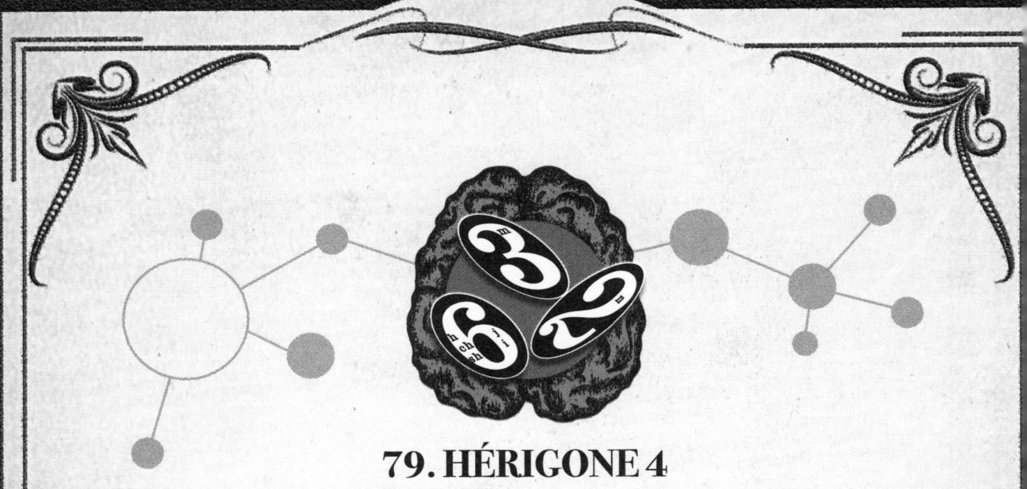

79. HÉRIGONE 4

For the first, chaining together a toff, a tear, a tub, and a tome took about a minute. I'll reveal this one; the toff was weeping, his tears filling his bathtub and overflowing to destroy his book. For the second, I linked together neigh to loo, to ma, to foe, to key, to jaw, to zoo, to bee. Seven separate mnemonics to remember. It took me about five minutes to get it all straight in my head. Finally, for the third number, I eventually had to settle for 49 58 31 60, which I expanded out to Ruby, Life, Meat and Cheese. By the time I'd come up with associations and linked and memorised those, something like fifteen minutes had passed. You may have done better of course, but I at least considered Holmes's point made.

80. JUGGED

While you can get close – you'll be 99% of the way there after 7 operations – it's functionally impossible to get to exactly half and half without pouring the entirety of one jug into the other and then splitting the result. Mathematically, it is equivalent to the sum of series of increasingly small fractions – 1/2 + 1/4 + 1/8 + 1/16 + ... – approaching but never reaching 1. More naturally, think of the two jugs as having a certain concentration of milk. One is higher, one is lower. When you pour from the higher to the lower, because you are only adding liquid of the same concentration as the higher to the liquid already in the lower-concentration jug, you will never be able to bring it all the way up to the same concentration as the higher. This is most obvious in the first pouring of milk into water. You are adding half a pint of 100% milk to a whole pint of 100% water, so of course the resulting mix will not be 100% milk. In the return, you are adding half a pint of 33% milk to half a pint of 100% milk, so of course the result will not be a pint of 33% milk. You can keep closing the gap, but you'll never get there exactly.

81. WAVY

"Ah, but light does diffract around corners," Holmes told me, after I eventually offered some sort of fumbling guess as to why it did not. "Diffraction however requires the obstacle to be the same order of magnitude as the wave it is obstructing. Sound waves are feet long, so corners are the right sort of size. Light is a far, far smaller wave, so its diffraction is only visible at microscopic levels."

82. PENNIES

If Wiggins is taking out 20 coins, then six must be left. If he then holds at least one ha'penny, he must have 6+1 = 7 of them. Similarly, he must have eight pennies, and eleven tuppences. Since 7+8+11 = 26, that's all the money he has. So he has 11*2 = 22p in two-penny bits, 8p in pennies, and 3.5p in half-pennies, for a total of 33.5p – rising, of course, to 45.5p when you include my poor shilling.

83. STAINLESS

The steel is alloyed with a significant amount of chromium – more than 10%, and in some cases more than 30% – and often other elements as well. The chromium reacts with the air to form a very thin protective coating that keeps the oxygen from reaching the iron molecules in any noticeable quantity. Since it is generated by the chromium throughout the metal, this coating is self-repairing.

84. SMITHS

The chance of meeting one blue-eyed girl if there are x blue-eyed girls and y girls in total is x/y. The chance of meeting a second, removing the first from your counts, is therefore (x-1)/(y-1). So the chance of meeting a pair who are both blue-eyed is these chances multiplied together, or x*(x-1) / y*(y-1). We know that this equation has to come out at 0.5, because there's a 50% chance of meeting two blue-eyed sisters, and we also know that x has to be at least 2, and y has to be at least 3. So try putting some numbers into the equation. With x at 2 and y at 3, the equation becomes 2*(1)/3*(2). The 2s cancel out, and we're left with 1/3, which is not 1/2. Changing y to 4 gives 2*(1)/4*(3), or 2/12, which is even less than 1/3. There must be more than two blue-eyed sisters. The next possibility is x=3 and y=4, for 3*(2)/4*(3). Again the 3s cancel out, leaving 2/4, or 1/2. So the correct answer is that the Smiths have four daughters, three of whom have blue eyes.

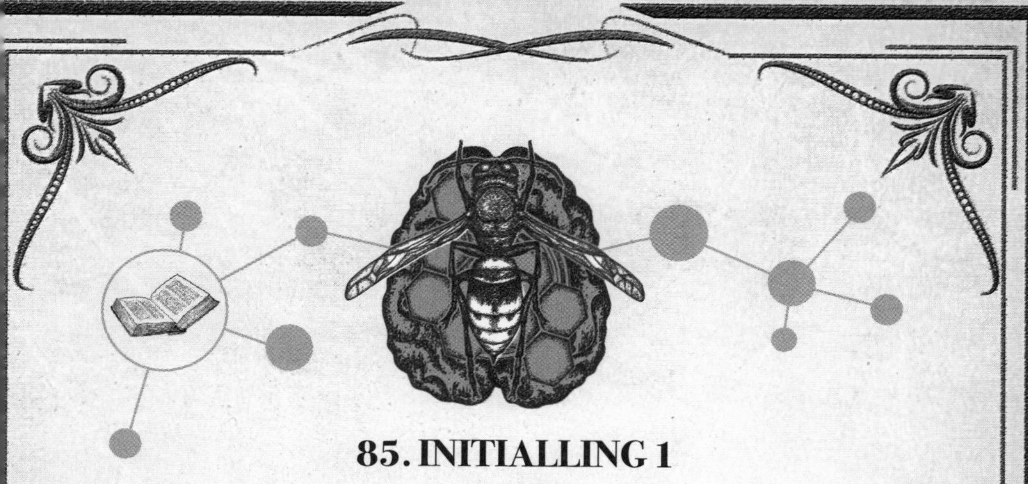

85. INITIALLING 1

Initialling out the speech gives you the following:

F, R, c, l m y e;
I c t b C, n t p h.
T e t m d l a t;
T g i o i w t b;
S l i b w C. T n B
H t y t C w a;
I i w s, i w a g f,
A g h C a i.

H, u l o B a t r -
F B i a h m;
S a t a, a h m -
C I t s i C f.
H w m f, f a j t m:
B B s h w a;
A B i a h m.

86. RACE

Holmes was correct, the answer – when I found it – was indeed simple: make the sons race on each other's horses, so that the first man across the line would inherit.

87. ROSEMARY

To come up with any sort of answer, we need to bear in mind what each boy knows. Alf can't have the number 1, because otherwise he'd know Simon had to have 2. So when he first says he doesn't know the other boy's number, then he's confirming that he doesn't have 1. If Simon had 1, he'd then know Alf's number, but he doesn't. But Simon doesn't have 2, either. If he did, and he now knew that Alf didn't have 1, then he'd know for sure that Alf had 3. So, so far, we know Alf doesn't have 1, and Simon doesn't have 1 or 2. Knowing this gives Alf enough information to deduce Simon's number. If Alf had 4 (or more), it wouldn't give him the answer, because if he had 4, Simon could have either 3 or 5, which are both possible. This can only mean that Alf has 2 or 3, since he now knows Simon's number. Remember that Simon can't have 1 or 2, as we've established. So either Alf has 2 and Simon is only left with 3, or Alf has 3 and Simon has to have 4. We can't tell which, but, either way, 3 is one of the numbers for certain.

88. BROTHERS

Ask him, "Are you the truth-teller?" The real truth-teller will know he is, and honestly answer "yes". The liar will believe that he is the truth-teller, and lie to you with 'no'. This hinges on the fact that the "you" here is doing double-duty, so the question is not precisely identical if asked to both, despite having the same wording. To the liar, it signifies the liar; to the truth-teller, the truth-teller.

89. WRONG TROUSERS

You need to think of your trousers as being akin to a tube. First of all, undo them and pull the waistband down over the legs, unpeeling them all the way off so that they are inside out on the rope. Then reach through from one leg hole all the way to the other leg hole, and pull them through themselves, turning them inside out again, so that they the right way round again. Because you unpeeled them to start with, the foot holes will be by your feet still. Finally, reach down each leg in turn, grab its foot hole, and pull it back up through itself. You will end up with the trousers inside out again, but this time with the waistband at your feet. Then you can put them back on normally, inside out. Why you'd want to do so in a situation of obvious extremis is quite beyond me, of course.

90. ST MARY'S AXE

It depends entirely on whether there are an odd or even number of balls in the bag. Going second does not help at all. There are slightly better odds of drawing a white ball after your opponent has pulled the first black ball, but those are exactly counterbalanced by the chance that your opponent would pull the white ball before you got your turn. Mathematically, if there were n balls at the start, the chance of getting the white first pick is a simple 1/n; the chance of getting it on the second pick is 1/(n-1) multiplied by the (n-1)/n cases where the first person didn't already win. The (n-1) cancel out, to give you an overall second-draw chance that is still 1/n. So if the total number of balls is even, it makes absolutely no difference. However, if there is an odd number of balls, and the game goes on as long as it possibly can, the person who went first will have one extra pick that the person going second will not get. It is a slight advantage, of course.

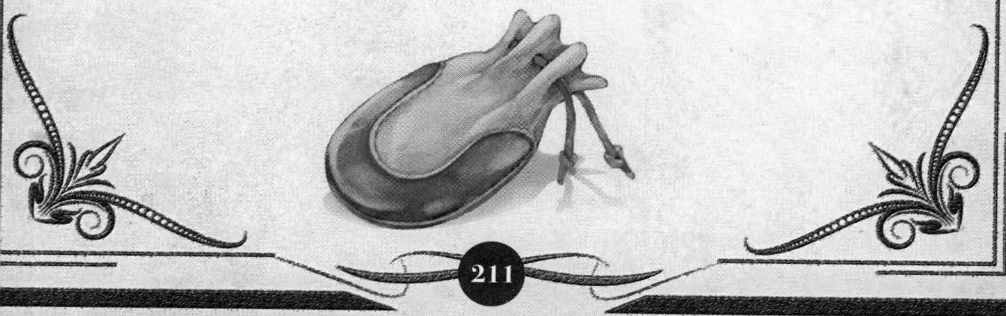

HARD

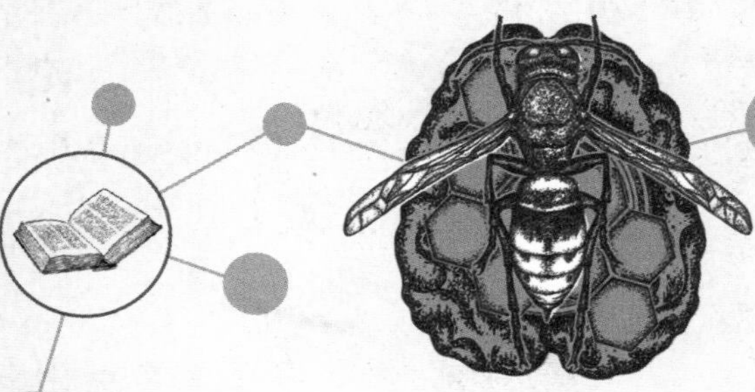

91. INITIALLING 2

The full text is:

Friends, Romans, countrymen, lend me your ears;
I come to bury Caesar, not to praise him.
The evil that men do lives after them;
The good is oft interred with their bones;
So let it be with Caesar. The noble Brutus
Hath told you Caesar was ambitious:
If it were so, it was a grievous fault,
And grievously hath Caesar answered it.

Cut down as Holmes suggests, it becomes:

F l e	S b T
I b t	H C
T m a	I s a
T o t	A C

92. BALLOONS

The half-inflated balloon is easier to blow into. As anyone who has inflated a balloon surely recalls, the initial inflation is significantly more strenuous than those which follow. This is due to the elasticity of the rubber, which strongly resists initial deformation. Past a certain peak, however, that occurs early in the inflation process, the resistance drops away until near the point of rupture, when it increases again.

93. FOUL

Borrell was forty-five feet behind the victim at night in a poorly-lit alley, yet somehow managed to see a small, thin weapon going up under the chin of a man facing away from him? Very unlikely, to say the least.

94. HOW MANY COWS

As the electricity from the lightning strike spreads out over the ground, it diminishes. If something or someone – a cow, in this instance – is making contact with the ground in two well-separated spots, the difference in the electric power between those two spots can set up a fatally significant voltage. So under the right conditions a cow that is, say, directly facing the point of strike might be killed by that power flowing through it due to the voltage disparity between front and hind legs, while another nearer to the strike but exactly square to it will be unharmed by the disparity between left legs and right legs.

95. AMAZING

All of them. There are a finite number of rooms, each of which has a finite number of states. More importantly, each room will eventually lead to each of its adjacent neighbours. Because of this, every room must be visited, given sufficient time. As this includes the exit room, escape is inevitable in every case.

96. MALFEASANCE

Rather than attempt to untangle the contradictions, with a set of reports this convoluted the best approach is to consider each of the eleven as the culprit in turn, and then look at how many of the statements are true or false in that event. For example, if John is guilty, then he, Gertie, Mark, James and Leonard are lying; if Gertie is the culprit, then John, Bessie, Simon, Mark, James and Flora are lying. But as we know than there are more than six liars, neither John nor Gertie can be guilty. There is only one option which produces more than six liars, which is if Donald is the guilty party. Then John, Gertie, Mark, Donald himself, Kitty, James and Flora are all lying, and Bessie, Simon, Fred and Leonard are telling the truth.

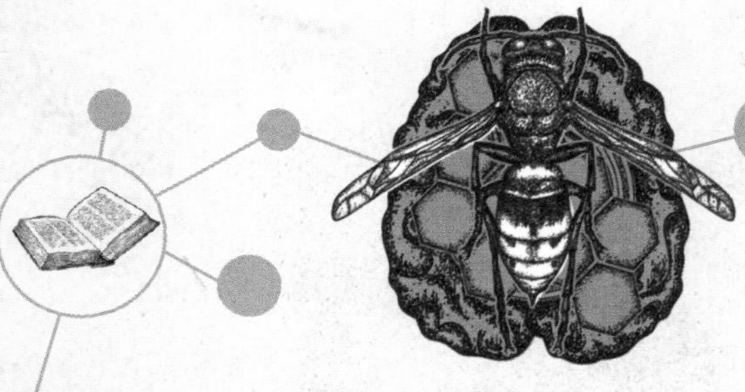

97. INITIALLING 3

The full text is:

Friends, Romans, countrymen, lend me your ears;
I come to bury Caesar, not to praise him.
The evil that men do lives after them;
The good is oft interred with their bones;
So let it be with Caesar. The noble Brutus
Hath told you Caesar was ambitious:
If it were so, it was a grievous fault,
And grievously hath Caesar answered it.

I turned the cut-down abbreviations into the following mnemonic images, attempting not only to use the letters but also allude to the lines themselves:

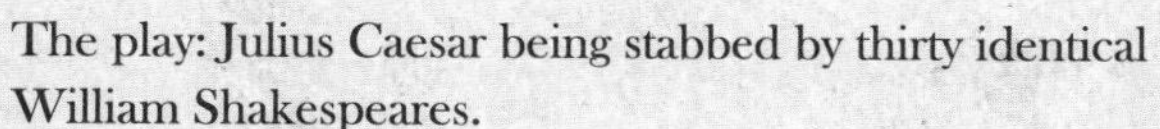

The play: Julius Caesar being stabbed by thirty identical William Shakespeares.

F l e: A flea with ludicrously huge rabbit ears.
I b t: A sibilant snake hissing its way over a coffin.
T m a: A knight Templar being followed by an ancient, ghostly evil.
T o t: A tiny tot, still in its mother's arms, radiating goodness.
S b T: A calm sabbath morning as exemplified by the Sunday newspaper, with a headline about the nobility of Brutus.
H C: A Hackney cab, emblazoned with a sign explaining the ambition of Caesar.
I s a: A tropical island, with a deep geological fault-line running down its centre.
A C: An acacia tree in full bloom, deep in conversation with its neighbour.

It did take a certain amount of time to associate each image with its words and bed it in as a mnemonic, but once I had done so, I found I barely even needed to think of the list to have the words arise in my memory.

98. THIEVES

Thomas is of median dangerousness and stole the emerald from the middle sister, Sophie; Richard is the least dangerous and stole the ruby from the eldest sister, Francine; and Harold is the most dangerous and stole the diamond from the youngest sister, Anna.

Since Richard is less dangerous than the man who took the emerald, and the man who took the diamond was the most dangerous, Richard has to have stolen the ruby, and must be the least dangerous, and the sister who owned it was the eldest. Anna did not own the emerald, and since she is not the oldest, Richard cannot not have stolen the ruby from her, so she must be the youngest and have owned the diamond. We know the man who stole the diamond from Anna was a bachelor with no brothers or sisters, so he cannot have been Richard or Thomas, who are brothers-in-law. He must therefore be Harold, the most dangerous thief, and since we now know Harold stole the diamond and Richard stole the ruby, then Thomas, the thief of median dangerousness, must have stolen the emerald. Then, since we know that Anna was robbed by Harold, and that Thomas did not steal from Francine, that means Thomas must have stolen from Sophie, and Richard from Francine. That settles every matter.

99. LENS

A telescope is designed to be used with a completely relaxed eye – that is, with your eye's natural focus set to leave the rays of light parallel, sometimes referred to as a focal length of infinity. If you are looking at a near object, the eye focuses to the target's distance from you. Since the telescope requires your eye to focus (theoretically) infinitely, it is clearly not giving you a closer image. Therefore, it must be making the image larger.

100. ROBBERS

Derek's statement tells us the result, true or false, but Alexander's statement, that Liam is correct and Kendry is wrong, is the key. If Liam is correct, then Henry and/or James are right. If Henry is right, Edward must be correct; whilst if James is right, then again Edward must be correct. So, if Liam is correct, Edward is correct.

From what Liam says about Henry or James, then Francis and/or Graham are also correct. Ian said that either Francis or Graham are right, so if Liam is right, Ian must also be correct. But if Edward and Ian are both correct, then Kendry is also correct.

This means Alexander must have been wrong about Liam being correct and Kendry being incorrect. Since Alexander is wrong, Derek is also wrong, and his statement that Bernard is not the thief is incorrect. Therefore, Bernard must be the thief.

101. METEORIC

The overwhelming majority of meteors we encounter originate within the solar system. Deep space is extremely sparse. So set aside the direction of the Earth's travel with respect to the rest of the universe. Within the solar system, the Earth is moving around the Sun, and one side of it – the part between midnight and midday – is facing in the direction it is moving. The direction we are moving is the direction most collisions will occur in, because it is easier to collide with something moving towards you than it is to collide with something moving away from you. It's like running through rain – your face gets wetter than your neck. For this reason, meteors are significantly more common between midnight and midday – and, obviously, much easier to spot before dawn.

102. WIRE

Once Holmes explained, I saw how simple the matter was. He rolled the paper into a tube, and then compressed it with a series of pinches, starting at one end. First he pinched an end flat with one hand, and with the other hand, pinched just above the first pinch, as close as possible, but at 90 degrees to the previous pinch. With both hands held firm, he forcefully pushed the two pinches together to sharpen the crease. Then he released the lower pinch, and repeated the process – rotate 90 degrees, pinch, compress together – all the way to the top of the tube. When unrolled, it had been imprinted with the pattern. I tried it myself. It took a couple of tries to get the knack of making it precise, and it's a little awkward to do behind your back, but it is surprisingly effective for perplexing an unwary colleague.

103. PALACES 1

Friends, Romans, countrymen, lend me your ears;
I come to bury Caesar, not to praise him.
The evil that men do lives after them;
The good is oft interred with their bones;
So let it be with Caesar. The noble Brutus
Hath told you Caesar was ambitious:
If it were so, it was a grievous fault,
And grievously hath Caesar answered it.

104. COINING

The answer I eventually settled on was: "You won't give me either the copper coin or the silver coin in return for this statement." This is true either if I get no coin at all, or if I get the gold coin. But in the former case, a true statement earning no coin would be inconsistent with the rules, so I must be given the gold coin for the rules to not be broken.

105. LOAD

It is easier to pull it, in fact. When you push it, part of the force you exert presses the wheel into the ground, making it more difficult to move. When you pull, you are removing that extra impediment.

106. FOUL

Miss Green was not inside the house when she saw the murder. She was returning from a walk in the grounds, and was a good forty yards from the building. Even so, she might have risked being seen and dashing for aid at the house, except that she could not be certain that the murderer was not, in fact, her butler.

107. DARK

It is not coincidental. In fact, many other moons in the solar system are also in lockstep with their parent planets – the Jovian moons Europa, Io, Callisto and Ganymede, for example. The effect is known as tidal locking. Whilst we all know about ocean tides, solid surfaces are also subject to tidal forces. They just don't flow around. The tidal forces between planet and satellite gradually slow the rotation of the faster until the two are in unity. The far side of the moon is not dark, incidentally. It is subject to the same shadowing from the Earth as the near side, only in opposite. When the moon is full, the far side is shadowed; when the moon is new, the far side is fully illuminated. Of course, neither side generates its own light, so as a matter of fact, I suppose it is all dark. But you take my meaning, I'm sure.

108. TESTAMENTAL

If each statement has a role to play, that means it must provide us with some useful information, and, therefore cannot be entirely irrelevant. Statements (a) and (c) are the relevant ones, and give us a clear solution – Nutty, Wilkins, Stinker. Permit me to explain. Statement (a) can be restated as "The person or persons who have eaten lobster with me in Southampton are to choose after Nutty." From this, we know that Nutty

cannot be last. Similarly, if (c) is relevant, the contenders for second must be Stinker and Wilkins. So Nutty must come first. Then, because (c) has relevance, Stinker must be the one to first grow a beard, and goes last, whilst Wilkins goes second. If (b) were to be relevant, it needs to be equivalent to "Stinker was not in Cirencester eight years ago, and the person or persons who have golfed with me on the first Thursday of one or more months go after the first man." But it does not add anything to (a) and (c), and neither (a) and (b) or (c) and (b) are sufficient to reach a unique solution.

109. FIVES

Well, we know the median is five, so both sets of numbers need to be x, x, 5, x, x. We also know that the range is 5, which means the highest and lowest have to be (0,5), (1,6), (2,7), (3,8), (4,9) and (5,10). But for the mean to be 5, the five numbers must sum to 25, and the highest possible totals of (0, x, 5, x, 5) and (1, x, 5, x, 6) are 20 and 23 respectively.

Similarly, (4, x, 5, x, 9) and (5, x, 5, x, 10) are too high. That leaves just

(2,7) and (3,8) as the min and max for our two lists, which are thus 2, x, 5, x, 7 and 3, x, 5, x, 8. From the mode, we know 5 must appear at least twice in each list. In the first list, 2+5+7 come to 14, so the remaining two numbers need to total 11. The possibilities are 5+6 and 4+7 – using 3+8 would fail the reach – so the first list is 2, 5, 5, 6, 7. In the second list, we are 9 short of 25, and we have the choice of 3+6 and 4+5. We need the second 5, so the second list is 3, 4, 5, 5, 8.

Therefore the solution is (2, 5, 5, 6, 7) and (3, 4, 5, 5, 8).

110. CHILDREN

We know there are four different numbers of children that sum to less than eighteen, and because more information is needed, we also know that they multiply together to produce a non-unique total. We'll call that number, Sally's house number, X. Because we don't actually need to know the smallest number of children, only that the number is important, that tells us that of the various ways of multiplying to X, one of them has a unique smallest number, and two or more of which have non-unique smallest number(s). If this was not the case, simply informing us about the importance of the number would either not be sufficient (no non-unique solution) or irrelevant (just one solution).

So the steps required to answer the problem are to list out all the possible options for four different numbers totalling 17 and under – from 1+2+3+4=10 to 2+4+5+6=17 – then multiply each option's component numbers together, and finally go through the list looking for one total with at least three possible options where one of those options has a set of component numbers which include one smallest number that is unique amongst the options..

The only multiple that fits the bill is 120, which has three possible sets of four factors totalling 17 or less – 1,3,5,8; 1,4,5,6; and 2,3,4,5. Of the three, only the last offers a unique smallest number. So the families have 2, 3, 4 and 5 children.

EMERSON

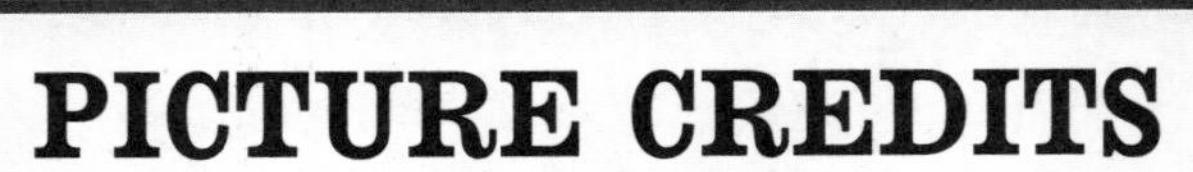

PICTURE CREDITS

The publishers would like to thank the following sources for their kind permission to reproduce the pictures in this book.

Key: T = Top, B = Bottom, L = Left & R = Right

Alamy: Baker Street Scans 14; /19th era 31

Dover Books: 15, 20 B, 38 TR, 48 TL, 48 TR, 65, 113, 164

Internet Archive Book Images: 30 R

Mary Evans Picture Library: 13, 21, 25, 29, 37, 39, 49, 51, 59, 79, 89, 90, 95, 103, 117, 127, 131, 139, 159, 166, 168, 169

Shutterstock: 9, 10, 11, 12, 18, 19, 26, 27, 28, 30 L, 32, 33, 36, 38 T, 38 TL, 40, 42, 43, 44, 46, 47 T, 47 B, 48 T, 50, 52, 53, 54, 55, 57, 58 TL, 58 B, 61, 62, 63, 64, 66, 67, 68, 69, 70, 71, 78, 80, 81, 82 TL, 82 T, 82 TR, 83, 84, 85, 86, 93, 97, 101, 102, 105, 106, 107, 110, 111, 112, 114, 115, 117, 119, 120, 121, 122, 123, 126, 128, 129, 135, 137, 141, 143, 144, 146, 147, 148, 149, 151, 152, 154, 155, 156, 158, 165, 167, 172

Wiki Commons: 35, 41, 45, 47 TL, 73, 75, 77, 87, 91, 109, 118, 125, 140, 145, 150, 153, 171

Every effort has been made to acknowledge correctly and contact the source and/or copyright holder of each picture and Welbeck Publishing apologises for any unintentional errors or omissions, which will be corrected in future editions of this book.